A Stranger in the Shadows

Joe climbed up until he could see over the edge of the roof. Through the darkness, he could make out someone kneeling in the shadow of the chimney.

Joe felt all his muscles tighten as he boosted himself up on to the roof. Crouching, he crept toward the kneeling figure. He held his breath as he moved nearer.

"Joe! What are you doing up there?"

When he heard Cody's voice from below, Joe was distracted for just a second, but that was one second too long. In a single fluid movement, the person beside the chimney stood up, wheeled around, and kicked.

Pain washed over Joe as the kick caught him in the stomach. Unable to catch his breath, he crumpled to the roof.

Joe gasped for air, then pushed himself to his feet. But his attacker had already scrambled down the fire escape and disappeared into the bushy woods behind the house.

The Hardy Boys Mystery Stories

Available from MINSTREL Books

For orders other than by individual consumers, Pocket Books grants a discount on the purchase of **10 or more** copies of single titles for special markets or premium use. For further details, please write to the Vice President of Special Markets, Pocket Books, 1230 Avenue of the Americas, 9th Floor, New York, NY 10020-1586.

For information on how individual consumers can place orders, please write to Mail Order Department, Simon & Schuster, Inc., 100 Front Street, Riverside, NJ 08075.

THE HARDY BOYS®

164

SKIN & BONES

FRANKLIN W. DIXON

A MINSTREL® BOOK

Published by POCKET BOOKS
New York   London   Toronto   Sydney   Singapore

This book is a work of fiction. Names, characters, places and incidents are products of the author's imagination or are used fictitiously. Any resemblance to actual events or locales or persons, living or dead, is entirely coincidental.

A MINSTREL PAPERBACK *Original*

 A Minstrel Book published by
POCKET BOOKS, a division of Simon & Schuster, Inc.
1230 Avenue of the Americas, New York, NY 10020

Copyright © 2000 by Simon & Schuster, Inc.

Front cover illustration by Jeff Walker

ISBN: 0-671-04761-2

First Minstrel Books printing November 2000

10 9 8 7 6 5 4 3 2 1

THE HARDY BOYS MYSTERY STORIES is a trademark of Simon & Schuster, Inc.

THE HARDY BOYS, A MINSTREL BOOK and colophon are registered trademarks of Simon & Schuster, Inc.

Printed in the U.S.A.

Contents

SKIN & BONES

1 A Nasty Surprise

A hollow *click-clack* sounded above Frank Hardy as he pushed open the door to the shop. Eighteen-year-old Frank, who was six feet, one inch tall, felt something brush the top of his dark brown hair.

"Cody doesn't miss a trick," Frank's brother, Joe, said with a grin. His blue eyes focused on the bones hanging over Frank's head. Joe was an inch shorter and a year younger than his brother.

Frank reached up and tapped the mobile hanging above the doorway. Narrow white bones dangled on clear plastic cords from a small skull with hollow eye sockets.

The Hardys stepped inside the San Francisco shop called Skin & Bones and put down their travel bags.

"Hey, guys, you made it." Cody Chang strode across the room to greet the Hardys. He was twenty-four years old, with black spiky hair. He had a wide smile, and his dark brown eyes flashed with pride as he swung an arm in a wide sweeping motion. "So what do you think? Pretty cool, eh?"

"Who buys this stuff, anyway?" Joe asked as he pushed his blond hair back and leaned over a display case. Through the glass he saw bird claws curved into deadly points, twisting tubes of shed snake skin, and shiny, bright-colored fish fins.

"Artists, teachers, doctors," Cody answered, looking around the shop. Several people were poring over displays in cases and on the walls. "Some people use them for decorations and crafts. You'd be amazed. Excuse me for a minute." He stepped away to help a customer.

A couple of minutes later the *click-clack* of the bones mobile announced another visitor to the shop.

"Hey, Dad," Cody said, raising a hand in greeting to his father. Frank noticed the affectionate smiles that the Changs exchanged. He knew that Cody and his father had become very close after Cody's mother had died, ten years ago.

"Sergeant Chang," Frank said, walking over with Cody to greet the short stocky man. "Great to see you.

2

Our dad was really sorry he couldn't make this trip with us."

"Not as sorry as I am, I'm sure," Thomas Chang said, greeting the Hardys. "It would have been great to talk over old times with Fenton. The last time you were here Cody hadn't opened Skin and Bones, had he? Isn't it something?"

"It sure is," Joe said. He was examining one of the skeletons hanging behind the counter.

"Wait till you see the rest of this place," Cody said. "I live on the second floor, but the real fun's up on the third. That's where my lab is." Cody's eyes sparkled as if he had a wonderful secret.

"You're still planning to stay at my house, I trust," Sergeant Chang said to the Hardys. "The guest room and refrigerator are waiting for you."

"You bet," Frank said. "And thanks for the invitation."

"Did you rent a car?" Cody asked.

"No," Joe answered, coming over to shake hands with Mr. Chang. "We took the Airporter into town and cabbed over here."

"Exactly why I stopped by," Mr. Chang said. "I just got a new car, but I haven't sold my van yet. You can use it while you're here—if you want. I figured you two might like some wheels while you're in town."

"Totally cool," Joe said, taking the keys for the house and van.

The four chatted until Sergeant Chang's partner picked him up, and Frank and Joe decided to take off to get settled in, clean up, and change clothes.

"Okay, get out of here," Cody said, walking them to the door. "Say, would you guys like to meet me at the zoo? Two-thirty at the snack bar. I have to pick up a package there."

The boys agreed, and after getting directions to the zoo, took off for Sergeant Chang's in the van. "This reminds me of our van," Joe said, turning to check it out. "Except it's red, of course."

The Hardys had stayed at Mr. Chang's comfortable small home on the west side of town in the Sunset District before. They changed into jeans, T-shirts, and sweaters before heading out to meet Cody.

At about two-thirty Frank had parked the van and was wandering with Joe through the zoo toward the snack bar. Cody was waiting for them at one of the small tables. His brow was wrinkled as he gazed into the distance.

"Hey, guys," Cody greeted them. "It's about time. I'm starved. I haven't had lunch yet." The three walked up to the snack bar window. "So, did you get all settled in?" Cody asked as he ordered a burger and

4

fries. The Hardys ordered a shake each because they'd already eaten.

"Sure did," Joe said. "And it's great to have the van."

"We have some time to kill," Cody said as he gathered up his lunch. "My package won't be ready until four or so. Let's hang out for a while."

The young men took seats on a bench in front of the orangutans. The male orang lolled in a hammock, his huge body practically dragging on the dusty ground below. A rust red baby orang darted out from behind a tree, batting a ball around the play yard.

"So, what's in this mysterious package you're picking up?" Joe asked.

Cody didn't answer.

"Earth to Cody," Joe said. "Come in."

"Hmm? What?" Cody said. "Oh, sorry. Did you say something?"

"I asked what's in the package you're picking up," Joe said.

"Stuff for the store," Cody answered in a matter-of-fact way. "An ostrich skeleton, a couple of anaconda skins, a zebra skull, and the real prize—anteater claws."

"Do you get all your merchandise from zoos?" Frank wondered, shooing a sea gull away from Cody's fries.

"Not all of it," Cody answered. "Some comes

from game wardens at preserves and parks, some from farmers and ranchers, some from fishermen. I've got a whole network of suppliers all over the world."

The three finished up and dumped their trash in a bin. Then they wandered around the zoo until Cody's crates were ready. The Hardys helped him load the stuff into his SUV. "You're coming back to my place, right?" Cody asked.

"Yep," Joe answered. "I want the full tour of your building, especially the mysterious third-floor lab you mentioned."

"Okay," Cody said, climbing into his SUV.

"Say, is that pizza place near Fourth and Irving still in business?" Frank asked. "I remember it from the last time we were here. They had the best pepperoni I ever tasted."

"It sure is," Cody said, nodding.

"Great," Frank said, heading for the van. "We'll stop to pick up some stuff we can reheat later—if that's okay with you," he called back. Cody agreed enthusiastically.

Frank watched Cody pull away before guiding the van into the traffic on Sloat Boulevard. About fifteen minutes later, he was parking the car a few yards from Alma's Pizzatorium. The Hardys strolled around the neighborhood while their pizzas and ravioli were being baked. Wisps of fog floated in from the ocean, and the temperature seemed to drop ten degrees.

By the time they gathered up the food and headed back to Skin & Bones, the fog had become a dense watery veil, making everything appear dim and blurry.

Frank parked around the corner from Cody's, in the only space available. "I don't think he's here yet," Joe said as they made their way toward the front. "He didn't mention stopping anywhere, did he?"

"No," Frank said. He slowed down instinctively. "But you're right. There's only one light on in the whole building. It sure doesn't look like anyone's in there. Let's check the garage—see if the SUV's there."

Joe peered in through the garage door window. It was dark inside, but he could see the hulking outline of Cody's vehicle. "It's there. He must be inside somewhere."

After Frank tried the front door and found it locked, Joe pulled on the handle of the old-fashioned garage door. To his surprise, it started to lift up. He put the bag of ravioli on top of the pizza boxes Frank was holding and continued pulling on the garage door handle.

The wooden door creaked as it moved out and up.

Fringes of fog darted in through the opening, and Joe squinted his eyes a little to get a better look.

A shot of adrenaline slammed through him as the floor next to the SUV slowly came into view. There was no mistaking the crumpled form lying next to the driver's side door. It was Cody Chang!

2 Roof Rage

"Frank!" Joe said. "It's Cody. And he doesn't look good."

Frank dropped the food on the ground and followed Joe into the garage. As Frank knelt next to Cody's still body, Joe flicked on the light.

"Cody!" Frank called, carefully lifting Cody's arm to check his pulse.

"I'd better call nine-one-one," Joe said.

"No!" Cody mumbled, rolling his head from side to side. "No, don't call anybody. I'm okay." He pushed himself up to a sitting position and rubbed the side of his head.

"You've got a lump," Frank said, examining Cody's head. "And the skin's all scraped away. You might have a concussion. Are you sure you don't want to see a doctor?"

"Yes, I'm sure," Cody said firmly. "No doctor. I just got knocked out. It's not the first time. Don't worry, if I think I'm in trouble, I'll let you know."

Frank knew he couldn't make his friend go to a doctor, so he resolved to keep an eye on him for a few hours, just in case. "What happened?" he asked, leaning down to help Cody to his feet.

"Somebody must have been waiting for me when I got back," Cody responded. "As soon as I stepped out of the car, I got hammered." He shook his head. "The bones!"

Joe and Frank lunged for the SUV. "There's one crate missing," Joe reported.

Cody checked each crate, reading the codes on the outside. "Oh, man," he said with a moan. "The ostrich skeleton. They took the ostrich skeleton and the anteater claws."

"They?" Frank said. "More than one?"

Cody thought for a minute, then sighed. "I don't know. I just said that. I never really saw anyone. I wonder why they left the rest," he added, staring at the other two crates.

"Are you sure you're feeling okay?" Joe asked Cody. "How about an ice pack?"

"Yeah, I'm fine. But ice sounds good. Let's go inside." Cody led the way out of the garage and into his office behind the shop.

While Frank picked up the packages from Alma's Pizzatorium, Joe checked the garage door lock. "The lock is pretty rusted out, but it might have been jimmied," he told Frank as they made their way into Cody's office.

"Wow," Joe said when Cody flipped on the light. The office was a mess, with papers and files flung around the room.

Frank reached down and picked up one piece of paper with mud caked on it.

"Is that a footprint?" Joe asked, tilting his head for a different angle of the smudged shape.

"Might be," Frank said, "but it's not very clear. We could probably narrow it down to size but I can't make out a sole design. It would be pretty hard to trace."

"What's this stuff?" Joe asked, picking off a reddish brown crumb. "There seem to be dozens of these stuck in that mud. It's soft, kind of spongy."

"I think I know what it is," Cody said, taking the speck and slipping it under a microscope on the table behind his desk. "Yeah, I was right. It's redwood bark and it's fresh."

"Fresh? What do you mean?" Joe asked.

"I mean it's untreated—it actually came from a tree," Cody answered. "It's not a piece of a weather-proofed deck or some chip that's been treated to be garden mulch."

"So are there actually giant redwood trees in San Francisco?" Joe asked.

"There sure are—very special ones. The coast redwood grows only in a very narrow strip of Pacific coast in northern California and southern Oregon," Cody answered. "The largest concentration around here is in Muir Woods National Monument, about twelve miles north of the city. There's a small grove in the city in Golden Gate Park."

"That doesn't really help us pinpoint a suspect," Joe said, picking up more loose files. Frank pitched in, and soon they had everything stacked neatly on Cody's desk.

Cody slumped into a large carved chair and leaned his elbow on the desk. With a sigh, he propped his head on his hand.

"Do you have any idea who did this, Cody?" Frank asked, pulling up another chair.

"Not exactly," Cody said quietly. "I mean I don't know who it is, but it's probably the same person or people who've been causing other trouble lately."

"Tell us what's up," Joe said, perching on the corner of the huge desk. "Maybe we can help."

"Man, the last several months have been tough," Cody began. "I've had a couple of other burglaries. The first time they just took stuff from the shop while I was at a police benefit Dad had organized. I figured it was a routine burglary—you know, B and E—breaking and entering."

"How about the next time?" Frank asked.

"That was different. They stole a shipment that had just arrived. Wasn't even uncrated. I'll bet they were surprised when they opened one of the crates. It was full of skulls and jawbones. Not what the run-of-the-mill burglar wants to try to unload." Cody gave the Hardys a weak smile.

"Any money taken? Safe robbed?" Frank asked.

"Nope," Cody replied. "Just merchandise. And this is the first time I've ever been hurt or there's been any vandalism," he added.

"I'm not sure this was just vandalism," Frank suggested. "Whoever did this might have been looking for something specific. You need to go through your files and papers to try to figure out whether anything's missing."

"Are those the only problems you've had?" Joe asked.

"No," Cody said. "At first I didn't think this other deal was related, but now I'm not so sure."

"What other deal?" Frank asked, jotting a few notes in a small pocket notebook.

"I've had trouble with shipments not arriving. Stuff mysteriously getting lost—some of it very special merchandise from faraway suppliers. That's been a real problem."

Cody stood up and began pacing behind his desk. "My business is different. I can't just order things the way a traditional store owner does and have them delivered by a certain date. I have to take what's available from my suppliers or wait until nature takes its course."

"What do you mean?" Joe asked.

"Say someone wants a mountain lion skeleton for a museum," Cody explained. "I can't just go out and shoot one or have someone shoot one for me. I never kill animals or have them killed. I have to wait until one dies from natural causes."

"The orders that were lost in transit were special orders for the same guy," Cody continued. "One I'd been waiting for for a couple of years. So I lost not only the shipment, but one of my best customers."

"And you think the lost shipments weren't really lost?" Joe asked. "You think they were stolen or something?"

"I sure do," Cody said firmly. He stopped pacing

14

and glared. "One shipment lost, maybe two. But three in five months? I don't think so."

"What did the freight carrier say about it?" Frank asked.

"Just what you'd expect: 'Sorry—file a claim.' Each time the order was changed to a pickup instead of a delivery. Not a pickup here in San Francisco, but one somewhere between the point of origin and here."

"Who changed these orders?" Joe asked.

"No one knows. It was all done on computer. The crates were signed for by someone using my name—I have copies of the receipts." Cody rummaged around in a desk drawer and pulled out three orders with his signature at the bottom.

Frank studied them. "Do these look like your signature?"

"One of them is kind of close," Cody said, "but it doesn't really matter. I'm talking about someone picking up one of my orders on a dock in Indonesia or a village in Nairobi. I sent the freight company my signature and asked them to send a copy to everyone along the shipping route, so signatures could be checked against it. But it didn't do any good. And it probably wasn't too smart, anyway. Now my signature is floating around the world, so anyone can copy it."

Frank scanned the receipt. He had the feeling

Cody was holding something back, that he had more to tell.

"Um, there's one more thing," Cody said as if reading Frank's mind. "Someone's been hacking into my computer and leaving threatening messages."

"Whoa," Joe said. "Like what?"

"I've got some printouts upstairs," Cody said. "I'll show them to you."

The three went up to Cody's apartment. A large living room stretched across the street side, over Skin & Bones. Behind the living room was a kitchen with an eating area at one end. A short hallway led to a bedroom and a large bathroom.

Frank and Joe settled at the dining table while Cody got the printouts of the threatening messages. Over heated pizza and sodas, the three looked at the pages. "As you can see, they're pretty standard stuff," Cody said.

"I'm watching you" was written on one. Others said, "You can't escape" and "Close Skin & Bones or you'll be sorry."

"Boy, there aren't any clues on these at all," Joe said.

"They're hacked in, so there's no originating address or number or anything," Frank pointed out.

"You guys met Dave Cloud the last time you were

out here, didn't you?" Cody asked. He waited while Frank and Joe nodded. "He and I used to be partners. He's started an online computer supply and equipment auction site."

"I remember him," Joe said. "He was a pilot and a technical wizard."

"That's him," Cody said. "I told him all about this. He's going to try to trace the hacker."

"What does your dad say?" Frank asked.

Cody gulped a big slug of soda and shrugged his shoulders. "I haven't told him. Look, he seems okay with everything now, but he was totally against the store at first. He wanted me to be a cop or a government agent or something like that—follow in his footsteps, you know? He was afraid I'd go bust with the store. If I tell him what's happening, all his worry genes will kick right in."

"But you've reported the burglaries to the police, right?" Frank asked.

"Sure," Cody answered. "Dad knows about them, but we both thought they were standard breaking and entering, like I said. That was before the other stuff happened. I haven't told him about the intercepted shipments or the computer hacking. I want to be able to handle it myself."

"We'd be glad to help," Frank offered.

"I was hoping you'd say that," Cody said. "Your being here is great timing."

"Hey, three heads are better than one," Joe said, grabbing another slice of pizza. As he took a bite, he heard a noise outside.

He sat up, his ears straining. "Shhh," he cautioned the others. "I heard something."

The three sat still. Then Joe heard it again, an odd grating, like metal rubbing against metal. He put a hand up, gesturing to the others to stay put. Carefully, he inched his chair back and walked to the kitchen window. It was very dark outside.

Joe quickly made his way down the stairs to the first floor and into Cody's office. His ears tuned to all outside noises, he quietly unlocked a door at the side of Cody's office. The door opened onto a narrow passageway between Cody's building and the one next door.

There was a wooded lot behind Cody's building—a dark area of trees and large bushes. Joe stood still, listening. This time he heard something from above. Stepping away from the house, he looked up. Someone was moving on Cody's roof.

Joe watched the shadowy form darting back and forth. He strained to see who it was, but it was too dark. He sprinted down the narrow passage to Cody's fire escape at the rear of the building. He lowered the

18

bottom ladder inch by inch, trying to keep the metal from scraping.

At last it was down and he was able to scale the ladder. He climbed up until he could see over the edge of the roof. Through the darkness, he could make out the back of someone kneeling in the shadow of the chimney at the far end of the roof.

Joe felt all his muscles tighten as he boosted himself up onto the roof. Crouching, he crept toward the kneeling figure. He held his breath as he moved nearer.

"Joe! What are you doing up there?"

When he heard Cody's voice from below, Joe felt as if his heart had stopped beating. He was distracted for just a second, but that was one second too long. In a single fluid movement, the person beside the chimney stood up, wheeled around, and kicked.

Pain washed over Joe as the kick landed in his stomach. Unable to catch his breath, he crumpled to the roof.

3 An Enemy Is Loose!

Joe gasped for air, each breath causing a new ripple of pain through his body. He shook his head and pushed himself to his feet. I've got to stop that guy, he told himself.

As Joe sprinted to the end of the roof, he called out to Frank to stop his attacker. He was too late. The person had already scrambled down the fire escape and disappeared into the bushy woods behind the house.

Joe walked to the chimney and checked out the area where the person had been kneeling. He found nothing but a small mirror, which he put in his pocket, and climbed down the fire escape to join Frank and Cody. They agreed the mirror wasn't much of a clue.

The three went up to Cody's apartment and into the kitchen. "I'm feeling a little woozy," Cody said, pouring a glass of soda.

"It's time to get you to the doctor," Frank said. "No more arguments."

"We'll see," Cody said noncommittally. "Joe, can you give me a description of the guy who kicked you?"

"Well, I keep saying 'the guy,' but you know, it could have been a woman, I guess," Joe answered. "I didn't get much of a look at the person—dark pants and sweater, hair under a knit cap. I never saw the face at all. You might be able to get a toe print from my stomach, though," he added with a half-smile. He could still feel the spot where he'd been kicked.

"Cody, I get the feeling you have a suspect in mind—for *everything* that's happened to you," Frank said. "Have you got a name for us?"

"Mike Brando," Cody declared.

"Who's Mike Brando?" Joe asked. "And could he be the guy who got me on the roof?"

"Nope, not on the roof, but everything else maybe. When I first opened Skin and Bones," Cody explained, "Brando was one of my best suppliers. He told me he was a former game warden and had worked in animal parks and game preserves in Australia, Africa, and Brazil."

Cody put down his soda, then leaned back in his chair. The expression on his face showed that he was still angry. "He had the whole package—career records, references, a list of terrific contacts all over the world."

"That sounds pretty impressive," Frank said. "Did his references check out?"

"Yep," Cody said. "He'd started his own search business and offered to serve as my middleman to line up the best specimens."

"He'd be sort of a bones broker," Joe concluded with a chuckle.

"Exactly," Cody agreed with a lopsided smile. He ran a hand through his thick dark brown hair. "He—" Cody was interrupted by the sound of the door buzzer.

Cody checked his watch as he stood up. "Yikes, I almost forgot—Deb was going to drop by tonight to meet you guys."

"I'll get it," Joe said.

Joe went down and unlocked the shop door. Waiting outside was a pretty young woman in a long skirt and jeans jacket. Thick wavy blond hair cascaded around her face. "Hi, I'm Deborah Lynne."

"I'm Joe Hardy. Come on in."

He led her through the store and back up to Cody's kitchen. Cody introduced her to Frank, saying that

Deb was his new business manager and also helped out in the store. He quickly filled her in on what had happened earlier.

"So, what did the doctor say?" Deb asked, helping herself to a piece of now cold pizza.

"I haven't seen one yet," Cody said with a sheepish glance toward Frank and Joe. "I'm okay."

"Come on, Chang," Deb said. She took the pizza out of Cody's hand and slapped it onto his plate. "I'll take you to Dad's. At least he can check you out. My dad's a doctor," she told the Hardys.

"All right, all right, I'll go," Cody said with a grin. "I can't fight all three of you."

Deb drove Cody to her father's, and the Hardys headed back to Sergeant Chang's. As the brothers were getting ready for bed, Deb called to say her father had given Cody a clean bill of health, and Cody was already back home. They agreed to meet at Cody's for brunch at ten o'clock the next morning.

Tuesday morning was cool and damp, and the city was cloaked in thick fog. Deb arrived shortly after the Hardys. In his kitchen Cody was fixing a big platter of burritos and eggs, and Frank was relieved to see that he looked well and rested.

Over breakfast Frank got right down to business.

23

"So, let's finish our conversation from last night," he said. "Why do you suspect Mike Brando?"

"Mike's first deliveries were great," Cody explained. "He got stuff I'd had trouble locating because I didn't have his contacts. But then he offered to get things that I knew were illegal," he said, his expression troubled.

"Internationally restricted bones and skins," Deb added. "No one can buy or sell them."

"But at that point it was just my word against his," Cody pointed out. "Dad organized a sting, and Brando walked right into it. Man, was he mad. He swore he'd make us pay."

"Oh," Joe said, "so that's why you said he couldn't be the guy on the roof. He's in prison."

"Yes," Deb said. "But we figure he could have someone on the outside helping him."

"He definitely could be behind the computer messages," Frank pointed out. "He's not in for a violent crime. He'd probably be a good candidate for computer privileges."

"If it's not Brando, then I haven't a clue who it could be," Cody said, finishing his third burrito.

"Great breakfast, Cody," Joe said, leaning back in his chair.

"Agreed," Frank stated. "So, how about that tour of

your lab you've been promising, Cody. I want to see how your business works."

"That's right!" Cody said. "You've never seen Bug Central. C'mon—let's go."

"I'll open the shop," Deb said, and went down to welcome the morning's customers.

Cody led the Hardys up to the lab, which took up nearly the entire third floor. "Over here is all my media stuff," Cody said proudly. A wall of floor-to-ceiling bookcases was crammed with tapes, books, and CDs. "I've got videos and books about nearly every animal, fish, and bird in the world. Plus prehistoric life and fossils." More shelves held boxes and albums of photographs, neatly cataloged, filed, and labeled.

A second wall looked like one in an artist's studio. Shelves, pegboards, and tables were covered with brushes, wire scrapers, scissors, rulers, colored pencils, compasses, tubes of paint, display stands and easels, frames, and rolls of tape and wire.

"Here's where I do a lot of the final work," Cody said, seating himself on the stool in front of his drafting table. "This is my favorite part, really—doing custom work for a client or getting a display ready for the store."

A third area of the room looked like a science lab. A worktable with two sinks anchored the wall. Bunsen burners, cleaning fluids, microscopes, and other para-phernalia stood waiting for Cody.

The fourth wall was nearly covered floor to ceiling by stacks of crates and boxes. In the corner was a door with a hand-lettered sign: Bug Central—Do NOT Open!

"So, this is Bug Central?" Frank said.

"Yep," Cody said, chuckling. "My specimens arrive in different conditions. They're not always clean, white, and ready to go. Sometimes they still have bits—or even a lot—of flesh on them."

With a wide grin, Cody opened the door to a large closet. On one wall were shelves of fiberglass bins of different sizes. Four old refrigerators lined the other wall.

Cody led the Hardys to one of the larger fiberglass bins, which was clear and gave them a view of what was going on inside. A large skull lay on a bed of cotton batting. Swarming over it were thousands of tiny caterpillars.

"Meet my assistants," Cody said with a flourish. "The dermestid beetle colony."

"You're kidding!" Joe said. "This is amazing."

"Lots of museums around the world have used dermestids since the eighteenth century—sometimes whole rooms of them," Cody explained. "Nothing cleans a bone faster. Adult beetles lay eggs in the flesh on the bone. The larvae—the little caterpillars—hatch and eat the meat. Then they burrow into the cotton at the bottom of the bin as pupae, emerge as adults, and the cycle begins again."

"Totally cool," Frank said, watching the dermestids in action. "What kind of skull is this?"

"That's the zebra skull we picked up at the zoo yesterday," Cody said. "It was pretty clean. I put my buddies to work on it last night when I got back from Dr. Lynne's."

"And the refrigerators?" Joe asked.

"I have colonies in them, too," Cody answered. "I pick up old refrigerators. Hey, the price is right—and they're really secure. See, the trick is to keep the dermestids from 'bugging' out on their own."

Frank and Joe groaned at the bad joke.

"They'll eat anything organic," Cody continued, "so they're very destructive. They eat wood, so this room has paint that's toxic to them. In case any of the little critters get away, they won't be able to eat through the wood."

Cody and the Hardys left Bug Central and went back into the lab. "This is really great," Frank said. "Looks like you have everything you'd ever need here."

"And I love it," Cody said, his eyes sparkling.

"Sometimes I wish I could afford to hire all the help I needed to run the business. Then I could just stay up here and play."

Frank and Joe followed Cody down the two flights of stairs to the shop. A pretty young woman in her late twenties stood at one of the display counters, talking to Deb.

"I know you," Cody said. "You recently bought Reflections, the club next door. Sorry I haven't been over to welcome you to the neighborhood."

"Yes, I'm Jennifer Payton," the young woman answered. She was tall and looked as though she worked out regularly. Her golden brown hair was pulled back off her face, and she had a huge friendly smile. "And you can make it up by doing me a favor," she added. "I'm in charge of a fund-raiser for the Children's Shelter."

"That's this weekend, isn't it?" Cody said, nodding. "You're doing a haunted house at the Soxx Mansion. You've done a good job promoting it."

"Except I'm in a real jam," Jennifer said, "and if you don't help me out, we may have to cancel."

A frantic look came over Jennifer's face, and for a minute Frank thought she was going to cry. "What happened?" he asked.

"There was a plumbing disaster at the mansion over

the weekend," Jennifer answered. "There was a lot of water damage, and it can't be cleaned up by this weekend. Plus I lost most of my haunted house decorations. I'm sunk." She sighed. "Unless . . ." She looked at Cody with a pleading expression.

"I don't get it," Cody said. "What can I do?"

"Well, I had only two choices, really," Jennifer said. "Cancel or relocate the whole thing to Reflections. I decided to relocate. And that's where you come in. . . ."

"I think I get it," Frank said. "You need to borrow some things from Skin and Bones to replace your decorations."

"Very good deduction," Jennifer said. "Say, you'd make a great detective!"

Frank and Joe grinned at each other.

"So, will you?" Jennifer pleaded. "Will you lend me some skeletons and shark jaws and other scary stuff? Please? It's for a good cause."

"Of course," Cody said. "Glad to help. We'll even help you set the stuff up."

"Thanks," Jennifer said, looking around the shop. "Some of this will be perfect."

"A haunted house, hmm?" Joe said. "Do you need any help *during* the event?" he asked. "Ticket-taker? Monster? Ghost?"

"Always room for more volunteers," Jennifer answered with a grin. "I've got the perfect costumes for all four of you. You can pick them up when you bring over the bones."

Jennifer bustled out the door, and Deb returned to tending to Skin & Bones customers.

"I want to take a look at the records of your transactions with Mike Brando," Frank told Cody.

"Last night when I got back from Deb's dad's, I sorted through all that stuff we picked up last night. So everything's better organized than usual. I can easily get the Brando stuff."

"Could you tell whether anything was missing?" Frank asked. "Records, receipts, whatever?"

"Nothing that I could tell," Cody said. "Maybe it *was* just vandalism."

"I don't know," Frank said. "One target was obviously the packages from the zoo. The lab wasn't touched, but it looks like the person wanted something from your office." Frank found it hard to hide his frustration. "Did Brando have an associate or anyone working with him when he was legitimate?" Frank asked as they shuffled through the papers.

The phone rang before Cody could answer. "Dave, what's up?" he said into the phone. "You're kidding! When?" Cody started pacing. Frank could see that Cody was getting angrier by the second. "I don't believe it," Cody said. "He had two more years. Okay, see you then. Thanks for calling."

Cody clicked off and turned to the Hardys. His dark brown eyes seemed to be shot through with darts of anger. "That was Dave Cloud. He's about three minutes away," he said. Cody's voice was very low, and his lips were pulled into a thin line over his mouth.

"It's making sense now," he continued almost to himself. Then he remembered Joe and Frank. "Mike Brando's out. He was released yesterday morning."

4 Clang, Clang . . . Crunch!

"Mike Brando's out," Joe repeated. "He had to be the one who decked you last night. He probably came here straight from prison."

"I wonder if your father knows he's out," Frank said. "He might be able to find out what his plans were for after prison."

"I'll talk to him later," Cody said. "Boy, it's all coming together now. It's no coincidence that I'm attacked the day Brando is released from prison."

"And you think the person who kicked Joe on the roof was also Brando, right?" Frank asked.

"I sure do," Cody answered.

"Who are we talking about?" came a strong voice from the door into the office.

"Hey, Dave," Cody said with a broad smile. Cody turned to the Hardys. "Guys, you remember Dave."

Dave greeted the Hardys while Cody got everyone a soda from the small refrigerator in the corner. Dave took a seat next to Cody's desk. He was tall and slim, with long legs, and moved loosely, like a basketball player.

"So, who are we talking about?" Dave repeated with a friendly smile.

"Mike Brando," Frank answered.

"That loser," Dave said, his smile vanishing. "Imagine letting him out for good behavior. He doesn't know the meaning of the term."

The four talked a while longer about Brando and his past crimes. When Dave finished his drink, he announced he was ready to go to work. "Let me at that computer, Cody. I'll see what I can find out about those e-mails." He pulled a computer disk from his pocket. "I wrote a program for you, which I'll load while I'm here. If you get any more threats, this will make them easier to track down."

While Dave worked on Cody's desktop computer in the office, Frank and Joe took the records of the interrupted merchandise orders and the files of the suppliers involved up to the lab and went over them with Cody. Frank also checked out the suppliers

33

through the Internet, in case there was any information about them that would lead him to the person who had ripped Cody off. He ran into one dead end after another.

Joe concentrated on learning how Cody developed his vendor leads to see whether there was a pattern that might allow someone access to the orders.

Cody went back and forth, from learning the new software from Dave, to helping Deb with customers in the shop, to answering questions for the Hardys. Dave poked his head in the lab at about four o'clock to say goodbye and agreed to return the next evening to go out for dinner. Deb left, and Cody closed the shop around six o'clock.

"I'd like to head back to your father's," Frank told Cody. "With the news about Brando getting released, this would be a good time to ask him a few questions."

"Okay," Cody said. "But remember, you promised not to tell Dad everything that's been happening around here. When we solve the case, then we'll tell him."

"You know, Cody, he could be a big help to us," Joe pointed out.

"I know, I know," Cody said. "But I'm not ready to confide in him yet. Let's give it another day or two—see what we can figure out."

"When to tell your father will be your decision," Frank agreed.

"Good. Say, I'll pick up something for dinner and meet you at Dad's."

As they drove to Sergeant Chang's, Joe and Frank talked about the person on the roof. "I know Cody thinks it was Mike Brando," Frank said. "But what would he be doing up there? Especially if he'd just clobbered Cody and ripped off those packages."

"Well, if he was interrupted when we came on the scene, maybe the roof was just a handy place to hide." Joe was silent for a minute. "No, that doesn't make sense. It would have been easier to hide in that wooded lot behind the shop."

"It would have been even easier to just get out of there," Frank said as he pulled into Mr. Chang's driveway. "I mean, why hang around at all? It doesn't make sense."

The Hardys and Cody's father talked about Mike Brando while they waited for Cody to arrive with dinner. Frank and Joe were both careful to keep their promise not to tell Mr. Chang specifics about the problems his son had been having.

After talking about Cody's business dealings with Brando, Frank steered the conversation to the prisoner's release the day before. "Cody was surprised that Brando was released so soon," he said.

"Well, I was, too," Sergeant Chang replied. "But that's the way things work nowadays. He apparently was a model prisoner, so he got time off for that. And they counted his time served while waiting for trial. He didn't make bail because the judge set it too high. The court figured that with all his international contacts, Brando could have easily skipped the country. I agreed with that."

"Are you worried about the threats he made when he was sentenced?" Joe asked. "Cody told us Brando said he'd make both of you pay for catching him in that sting."

"Well, it's always wise to be cautious about any threats," Sergeant Chang said.

"About any what?" Cody asked as he walked in with sacks full of dinner for the four of them.

"We were talking about Mike Brando making good on his threats," Frank said.

"That's right, son," Mr. Chang agreed. "I've talked to several people, and the consensus is that Brando'll head north to his sister's in Seattle."

The Hardys helped Cody lay out the white paper cartons of steamed buns, aromatic chicken, beef with garlic almonds, sticky rice, and sweet-and-sour ribs.

"Brando behaved himself in prison," Mr. Chang added, taking his seat at the dining room table. "Even took some computer training."

Frank and Joe exchanged glances as Cody changed the subject. "I showed the guys Bug Central today," he told his father.

"That's really something, isn't it?" Cody's dad said, chuckling.

"Unbelievably cool," Joe said. "Sort of like the ant farm I had when I was a kid—only on a galactic scale!"

"There's something weird when you think about all those fuzzy little guys, crawling over bones, munching away," Frank said.

"I know," Cody said. "Don't you love it? Some museums have used them to clean off whole elephants or giraffes. One Canadian museum's beetle colony specialized in whale carcasses."

Frank, Joe, and Cody told Sergeant Chang about Jennifer Payton's request and the upcoming haunted house fund-raiser.

After dinner Sergeant Chang told them he was having trouble with the starter on his new car. Joe offered to take a look at it, so Cody's father and he went out to the garage. Frank and Cody cleared off the dining table.

"My dad's one of the best detectives around," Cody told Frank. "But he didn't know Mike Brando as well as I did, and I can't believe that Mike has changed that much. That man seemed to be born without a conscience."

The Hardys, Cody, and Mr. Chang stayed up late talking so Cody decided to stay over at his dad's that night.

Wednesday morning Sergeant Chang's car wouldn't start at all. He said he'd take a bus to work, but Frank insisted he use his van. Sergeant Chang agreed, saying he'd get his car fixed and the van over to Skin & Bones later that afternoon.

Joe drove Cody's SUV away from Sergeant Chang's, with Cody in the front passenger seat as navigator and Frank in the back. "I've got a couple of stops to make on the way back to the shop," Cody said. "I need to pick up my new flyers and some skeleton chains. Take the next left."

"Hey, guys," Joe said as he turned on to Geary. "Looks like we may have picked up a tail."

"Someone's following us?" Frank said, sneaking a peek out the back window.

"The dark green sedan," Joe said, periodically checking his rearview mirror. "He's been with us since we left."

Joe carefully wove in and out of a couple of lanes and drove completely around one block. He watched the green car follow each move at a distance.

"There's the printer's," Cody said, pointing to a storefront on the right. "You can stop in the loading zone for a few minutes while I get my stuff."

Joe pulled into the loading zone. They all watched as the dark green car slowed down, then suddenly sped up, cruising past them.

"Did you see the driver?" Cody asked. "He went by so fast, I didn't get much."

"Dark nylon jacket—black or maybe navy blue," Joe said. "Wraparound shades, black knit ski cap pulled down over the ears, gloves."

"I couldn't tell whether it was a man or woman," Frank said. "Could it have been the person on the roof, Joe?"

"Yeah," Joe said. "It could have been. Let's split up," he added suddenly. "I want to go after that guy. See you back at the shop."

Frank and Cody jumped out of the SUV, and Joe took off after the green car.

After they had picked up the flyers, Frank and Cody headed for the metal craftsman's studio to get some of the special chains that held up the skeletons at Skin & Bones.

Frank and Cody walked a few blocks to a cable car stop. Within minutes they were climbing a series of very steep hills in the rumbling, clanging car.

When they reached the top of the third hill, at a very busy, noisy intersection full of cars and pedestrians, the cable car stopped. A lot of passengers got off and even more got on before it started the steep descent down the other side of the hill.

Frank was sitting at the front end of one of the open benches that ran along the outside of the cable car. He could see far down the hill to Fisherman's Wharf. In the distance, the prison Alcatraz sat on an island in the bright bay.

The cable car gripman clanged the familiar bell, alerting everyone that the car was about to move. There was a final flurry as last-minute passengers hopped aboard, elbowing one another.

Frank and the others already on the car were jostled in the frantic rush. Suddenly, someone inside the car shoved Frank's shoulders forward so he was leaning out over the street. He started to turn around to complain, but he was rammed again from behind—this time in the middle of his back.

Before Frank could get his balance, he lurched out of his seat. He flew forward until his forehead scraped the ground. He realized that he was only half on the street—the rest of his torso and legs were hanging over the cable car footboard.

He tried to roll off completely, but a sharp pain in his ankle stopped him. With a sickening feeling, he realized his foot was caught in the vertical handrail attached to the front corner of the cable car.

In the din of the traffic, he heard Cody call his name. He doesn't see me, Frank realized. He can't see where I am!

Frank twisted and turned, trying to get free, but each move inched him farther around the front of the cable car and closer to danger. He called back, but the noisy intersection swallowed up his yells. He felt the cool slickness of metal against his cheek and realized his head was resting on one of the tracks. His pulse seemed to tear through his throat as he heard the grinding scrape of the grip lever.

Clang-clang. Frank's heart seemed to stop as the loud bell noisily announced that the cable car was about to move.

5 The Suspect Slips

Clang-clang, clang-clang. The sound of the cable car bell cut through the air again. The busy intersection was crowded with cars and pedestrians. Over the din, Frank could hear Cody calling his name. He could also hear a few people yelling at the gripman.

Either the gripman couldn't hear or it was too late because Frank could feel the rumbling vibration of the car as it began to move downhill.

Twisting and sliding, Frank struggled to pull his body up so he could free his leg with his hands. The vertical handrail that had his foot trapped was nearly within reach. Calling on all his strength, he strained to raise his shoulders and head until he was almost sitting. With a great gulp of breath, he flung his arm out and grabbed for the handrail.

The feel of the cool steel rod in his palm renewed his energy and determination. "Cody!" he yelled. "Down here!"

"Frank!" Cody saw him at last. So did others on the cable car. Frank heard the grinding of the ratcheted lever as the gripman pulled it partway back. The jaws of the cable grip released its tight hold, and the cable car vibrated to a humming idle.

Frank and Cody worked Frank's foot out of its trap, and Frank hoisted himself back up on to the footboard of the cable car. He was bombarded with questions from the gripman and a few of the passengers.

"Are you really okay?" Cody asked after Frank had assured the others he was fine.

"Yes," Frank said, reaching down to rub his ankle. "Thanks for the assist."

"No problem," Cody said. "What happened, anyway?"

"I was pushed," Frank said in a low voice. "I'll tell you about it later."

Clang-clang. As the gripman prepared to close the grip jaws on the underground cable, Frank noticed a man in the shadows of an alley straight ahead. The man seemed to be staring at him. He was tall and built like a football receiver, solid and muscular. He wore sunglasses and a baseball cap pulled low over his face.

When Frank caught his eye, the man turned and quickly darted back down the narrow gap between two buildings.

"Looks like this is our stop after all," Frank said to Cody as he jumped off the cable car.

Frank's ankle complained painfully, but he kept running after the mysterious man.

"What's happening?" Cody called from behind, panting.

Frank didn't take time to answer his friend. His whole concentration was focused on ignoring his throbbing ankle and catching up with the man. At last the man was cornered in a courtyard. There was no way out of the courtyard except the way they had entered.

The man turned to face Frank, who watched carefully to see whether the man was carrying a weapon. He seemed to be unarmed. Still, Frank stayed on his guard.

As Frank and the man faced off, Cody ran into the courtyard. "Mike Brando!" Cody yelled.

Frank's nerves tingled—even more on alert.

"So?" Brando grunted. "It's me. So what?" His voice was deep and throaty. It sounded like faraway rolling thunder. He glared defiantly at Frank and Cody. It seemed as if he was daring them to take him on.

Cody took the bait. He started toward Brando, but Frank's arm shot out to hold Cody back. "Why are you following us?" Cody asked. "And why did you push Frank off the cable car?"

"What are you talking about?" Brando sputtered. "*I'm* the one being followed here. I'm standing around minding my own business and you two take off after me."

"Were you on the cable car back at that intersection?" Frank asked.

"And what about last night?" Cody asked. "Where's my ostrich?"

"Give me a break," Brando said. "What's happened to you while I was away? Sounds like you've gone a little crazy, Chang. I'd watch that if I were you. They might lock *you* up." Brando grinned at Cody.

Cody flew toward Brando again, but Frank managed to catch him before he got too far. "Don't do it, Cody," Frank warned. "Don't let him get to you."

45

"You're right," Cody agreed. "But let's call the po-lice—or my dad. We'll get to the truth then."

Brando's grin turned to a scowl. "Pay attention to your pal here, Chang, and back off," he snarled. "In fact, I think I'll give the cops a call myself. Seems to me *I'm* the one being bugged here."

Frank turned to Cody. "He's right," Frank said qui-etly. "We have no proof that he's done anything."

As Frank and Cody retraced their steps out of the courtyard, Cody couldn't resist a final jab. "Don't think you're getting away with anything, Mike," he called over his shoulder. Frank turned and walked backward, so he could keep an eye on Brando.

"You'll slip up," Cody yelled as they left the court-yard, "just like you did the last time."

"We've got to get that guy, Frank," Cody said as the two walked back to the cable car stop. "He's been out of prison two days, and he's already managed to attack us both."

"I agree that it's probably more than coincidence that he was standing a few yards from where I was pushed," Frank said. "But coincidence won't cut it. We need proof, Cody."

"But how are we going to get that?"

"Our best bet is to find out who interrupted your shipments and who's sending the threatening

46

e-mails," Frank answered. "You know, it might be time to tell your father about your suspicions."

"Maybe you're right," Cody said. "I want you and Joe to help, but it's not fair to put you in such danger."

"That's not what I mean," Frank said. "It's just that your father has contacts who could help. For example, he knew that Brando took some computer training. Your dad could contact the prison where Brando served time. Maybe they could check the hard drives of the computer he worked on. Even when you delete files, they're still in there somewhere. If Brando sent the messages to you from a computer in the prison, a trained technician might be able to pull them out."

"That sounds good, Frank," Cody said. "I see your point, but just give me a little more time. I'd like to see what we can find out first. Dave's been working on the e-mails. He might have something for us by the time we get back."

While Frank and Cody waited for the next cable car, Frank saw Mike Brando emerge from the alley and slink off into the crowd. Brando probably pushed me, Frank thought, but we've got to get some proof. I wonder how Joe's doing.

* * *

47

While Frank and Cody were narrowly escaping danger on the cable car and then confronting Mike Brando, Joe was pursuing his own lead.

When the brothers split up, Joe sped quickly after the dark green car he was sure had been tailing them. It took him a few blocks, but he finally spotted the car. Within minutes he settled in a few cars back, so the other driver wouldn't spot him.

Is this the same guy who nearly kicked me off Cody's roof? Joe wondered. Looks like the same kind of hat and jacket. Of course a lot of people wear that style.

"So why did you follow us from Sergeant Chang's," he muttered. "What do you want?"

Joe expertly wove Cody's car through the lanes of traffic, keeping his quarry in sight. He watched the dark green car pull into Golden Gate Park. Then the cars in front of Joe slowed as the light at the intersection ahead turned yellow, then red.

Joe pounded the steering wheel once in frustration. He watched the green car take the first left inside the park. Joe waited impatiently for the light to turn green again.

At last he was able to continue. He pulled into the park and turned left.

There were no cars on the street ahead of him. From the high seat of the SUV, he was able to scan over and around the cars parked along the street and within scattered parking areas. But nothing looked like the car he'd been following.

Finally he did spot the dark green sedan parked at the Polo Field. The area was very crowded, with lots of pedestrians ringing the track and filing into the Polo Field stands.

Joe drove around the area, searching for someone dressed in a dark jacket, wraparound sunglasses, dark knit cap, and gloves.

"Nothing," he muttered. Then suddenly Joe saw his quarry. The driver of the green car was headed for the stands along the side of the track.

One thing's sure, Joe thought as he parked the SUV and took up the chase on foot. This guy followed us from Sergeant Chang's, and I'm going to find out why.

But once again his target slipped away. Joe searched the polo stands for fifteen minutes but couldn't find the person. "I don't give up this easily," Joe muttered. "If I can't get you, I'll settle for the car."

He headed back toward the green sedan. He knew he'd have no trouble finding it if it was still there. It was parked at a sloppy angle, and Joe figured the driver had been in a big hurry.

49

As he walked toward the parking area, Joe felt a whoosh of air behind him. He turned just in time to see the person in the dark windsuit and knit cap drive by.

Only this time the person wasn't in the green car. The person was behind the wheel of Cody's SUV!

6 Ride to the Rescue

Frustration spilled into anger as Joe watched the man he'd been tailing drive off in Cody's car. "He must have hotwired it," Joe muttered, feeling Cody's keys in his pocket. He whipped around, looking for a police officer or a guard, but saw no one.

"Yes!" he finally said, spotting the large complex of buildings making up the Golden Gate Stables. Within minutes he had rented a horse and was saddled up and on the bridle trail.

The trail was nearly empty, so Joe made up time by galloping along in the direction that Cody's SUV had gone. When he met up with slower riders, he left the trail and carefully made his way along the street.

At last he spotted Cody's vehicle a block ahead,

weaving in and out of traffic, working its way toward the west end of the park. In the distance Joe saw the white foam of ocean waves beyond the park. A honking horn behind him drew his attention away for a second. He skillfully moved the horse back on to the bridle trail.

When he glanced back at the street again, he saw Cody's vehicle ahead. It was parked on the grass under a grove of cypress trees near the oceanside entrance to the park.

Joe rode slowly toward the car. He could see no one inside, so he guided the horse to a halt under the cypress grove. He dismounted and tied the horse to a small tree. Across the street a full-size windmill stood in a small garden. Its sails turned in the breeze from the ocean.

Cautiously, Joe approached Cody's car. It had been abandoned, the driver's door slightly open.

"What's this?" Joe mumbled, reaching inside the car. A set of keys on a simple brass chain protruded from the ignition.

Joe opened the glove compartment and found the owner's manual. Without touching either key, he pulled on the brass chain. The ignition key came out, and he dropped the two keys between pages of the owner's manual. Then he put the manual in his jeans pocket and closed the car door, locking it.

He ran quickly through the cypress grove, searching for the man who had stolen Cody's car. There was no one there.

Joe doubled back to the car and hurried out of the park to the open area stretching to the oceanfront.

A wide stretch of concrete, crisscrossed with parking lines, connected the park to the oceanfront street known as the Great Highway. A short cement wall separated the street and sidewalk from the low grassy dunes, the sandy shore, and the Pacific Ocean. The wind blew across the water, swirling sand up from the dunes and depositing it on the street and in Joe's eyes.

There were no cars on the street, and as Joe walked toward the beach, he noticed a sign. The street would be closed that afternoon, the sign said, so that the city could sweep.

Joe knew there would be no swimmers in the water. Posted warnings forbidding swimming warned of a dangerous current. But a few people were scattered along the wide beach. A mother and two children were building sand castles, a boy was walking his dog, several young women were sunbathing, a couple of older men were fishing, and a girl was pacing the sand with a metal detector.

Nobody in a dark windsuit, Joe thought as he gazed

down the beach in both directions. Sea gulls swooped and called, watching for their lunch to appear.

Joe ran back across the highway, uncomfortable about leaving the horse alone much longer. On his way he passed a hot dog vendor stirring a steaming bin with a long-handled spoon. Joe walked up to the vendor's cart.

"How ya doin', young fella—what can I getcha?" The vendor greeted Joe with a big smile topped by a bushy mustache.

"Some information, I hope," Joe said. "Did you see anyone run out of the park in the last few minutes?"

"Sure did," the vendor said. "You."

"Besides me," Joe answered. "Before I did. Dressed in a dark windsuit."

"Don't think so," the vendor said, looking around. He took off his hat and seemed to be thinking hard. "Nope. I had some customers about ten minutes ago. I was pretty busy with them, so I might have missed him."

Next Joe raced into the glassfront restaurant just outside the park entrance and asked the cashier the questions he'd asked the hot dog vendor.

"You know, I might have seen who you're talking about," the young woman said. "Was it a man or a woman you're looking for?"

"I'm not sure," Joe said. "Could be either one."

"That's what I'm thinking, too," the cashier said, nodding her head. "This person came tearing out of the park, looked around for a minute, then turned and raced back in. Seemed to be heading toward the windmill. But I couldn't tell you much more than that. I sure couldn't give you any kind of ID, if that's what you need."

"Thanks a lot," Joe said. "You've been a help." He sped back into the park. Glad I took Cody's keys, he told himself. Whoever it was must have realized there was no place to hide out here and ran back in to grab the SUV again.

Cody's car was still parked where it had been, and the horse was still tied to the cypress tree. From behind him, Joe heard the sails of the windmill creaking in the wind. Joe crossed over to the small garden of purple and orange flowers that surrounded the windmill.

The structure was fifty to sixty feet high, and each of the two crisscrossed sails looked as if it was nearly that long. As the sails came down, they missed the deck by only a couple of feet. As they climbed back up, the wind from the ocean wrapped them in greenish gray fingers of fog.

A third of the way up, a large overhanging deck with a railing encircled the stone-block building. A plaque near the windmill said that it had been built in

1902 to pump water to a reservoir and had been restored in 1981.

Joe walked around the sidewalk that circled the base of the windmill. A much smaller building stood at the end of a path in a wooded area. Joe reasoned that was probably a pumphouse or maintenance shed.

There were several window openings in the wall, some round and some rectangular. From where Joe stood, they all had been closed off with brick or cement, although his line of sight was partially blocked by the large deck above his head.

A few concrete steps led down to large double doors made of rusted steel in the base of the windmill. In the doors were two holes about four inches square. Joe looked through one and saw only a round dark room. A few paper cups and some leaves littered the floor. There were small piles of trash either blown in or thrown through the square holes.

Joe thought he heard a noise from inside but couldn't be sure what it was. Probably an animal or bird, he thought. But the twitch he felt at the back of his neck told him he ought to make sure.

He checked to see if he was alone. There was no one in sight. At this end of the park it was still damp and foggy—not ideal conditions for strolling.

Then he heard another sound. It was a woman's

voice, and it sounded as if it was coming from inside the windmill. He couldn't hear the words, but she seemed to be arguing with someone.

The double doors seemed to be held together by a rusted padlock. Joe glanced around again. Then when he checked out the padlock, he saw that it was attached only to the pin on the hasp of one door. Someone had gone in this way. He pushed on the door.

He held his breath and peered inside. It was very still within the dusty room. As he stepped inside, a waft of fog entered with him.

As Joe closed the door, the light was blocked out and he stepped into nearly total darkness. Only dim light filtering in through the two square holes and a sliver of light on the wall above gave him any bearings at all. A scratching scuttling noise above sent a wave of heat down the back of his neck.

His thoughts came quickly. There's a door or window up there to the deck. Whoever was in here heard me come in and stepped out onto the deck.

He heard the woman's voice again. It sounded as if she said "away," but then her voice was muffled.

I was right, Joe thought. She's out on the deck. But someone must be with her. And she doesn't sound too happy about that.

Joe squinted to get a clearer picture. He was very

cautious as he edged around the room, his back to the wall. He tried to remain calm, but his pulse beat faster and louder with each step. He knew he was an easy target. He looked around for something with which he could defend himself. This will have to do, I guess, he thought, reaching for a short plank of wood.

His eyes now used to the dark, he spotted something in the corner—a navy blue ski cap. He immediately thought of the driver of the green car. He picked up the cap and stuffed it into his back pocket. As he did, something slipped to the floor.

It was a small white cardboard disk, rimmed with metal, with the number 5773 printed on the front and the numbers 14-7-38-5-9 on the back. A small hole was punched through the top of the disk.

Joe scooped it up and jammed it into his front pocket. He inched on around until he reached a rough ladder made of wooden planks bolted into the wall.

Please don't creak, he thought as he stepped onto the lowest plank. There was no sound, so he continued climbing up toward the sliver of light coming from around the edge of the deck door.

Joe reached the last step and a landing next to the door. He could feel the chill of the fog as it wound in the opening and around him. Carefully, he scrambled up and onto the platform. With his back hugging the wall, he peered out through the narrow opening to the deck.

Outside, two people, both dressed in dark clothes, were struggling in a sort of slow-motion wrestling match. The whistling vibration of an approaching windmill sail penetrated the air. Joe strained to get a good view of what was happening before he took any action. Then he heard the young woman cry out. "Let go of me—now!"

Joe jumped into the action. "Hey," he yelled, slamming open the door. He stepped onto the deck, holding the plank high. He could see only the dark-jacketed back of one of the two people. That person whirled around. Joe's pounding heart nearly drowned out the sound of the approaching windmill sail.

The man facing Joe wore a ski mask. In an instant, he had lifted the young woman up and was holding her out, across the railing. He didn't speak, but his gaze dared Joe to come closer.

Joe looked at the woman in the dark purple windsuit. He was stunned when he recognized her. "Deb?" he said. "Is that you?"

Her reply caught in her throat and came out as half gasp, half sob.

Startled, the man glanced around. Then he suddenly dropped Deb and raced off.

When he let go of her, Deb was half sitting, half lying on the deck railing. The sudden release made her lose her balance. She flailed her arms, trying desperately to keep from rolling over the railing and onto the walkway below.

Joe rushed toward her, but he knew he couldn't make it in time. The adrenaline pumped through his veins as he yelled, "The sail . . . grab a sail."

Deb flung her arms toward the sail inches away. Her fingertips connected, and she hooked them through the gridwork that edged the wooden sail.

With a huge burst of energy, Joe lunged toward her, throwing himself at her toes as she was pulled up from the deck. Her slick leather shoes slid right through his fingers.

Deb stared down at Joe in terror as she disappeared into the misty cloud curling around the top of the windmill. Her scream seemed to blast the fog right into his face.

7 Busting Out

Deb's scream drilled into Joe's brain. His temples thundered as he saw her clinging to the windmill sail, rising higher and higher into the fog. As the sail moved, her legs swung wildly.

"Try to hold still, Deb!" Joe called. "And don't look down. Just hold tight. You'll be back around soon and I'll bring you in." In the distance he could see the man with the ski mask disappear into the woods.

The windmill sails were huge, but they creaked and shook as they carried their accidental passenger. They inched around, slowing to a crawl. For a moment Joe's breath stopped as he thought the windmill might halt completely, with Deb dangling far out of his reach.

But the crisscrossed wood kept moving, drawing its *X* in a huge circle.

"I'm still here, Deb," Joe called. "I'm waiting for you. You'll be off that thing soon. Just hold on."

As the sail moved, Deb's position changed. At first she was hanging off the bottom end of the sail, straight down. When it drew up so that it was horizontal to the ground, she dangled at a right angle to the sail.

"I can't do it," she yelled. She sounded very frightened. "I can't hang on."

"Yes, you can," Joe urged. "It's scariest right now, while the sail is horizontal. Soon you'll be hanging from the top of the sail, and you'll feel more support from it."

The sail carrying Deb moved toward the top of its arc. Joe could barely see her through the fog—she was so high, far above the treetops. The sails slowed to a crawl, then a stuttering halt. But with a shuddering tremor, they began moving again.

At last Deb was coming back down, moving around the circle. As she neared Joe, his pulse quickened. He knew he had only a few moments to rescue her. If he missed the opportunity, she'd have to go through the whole circuit again.

"I have to get her on the first try," he mumbled, pumping himself up with anticipation. "I don't think she can take another go-round."

"My fingers are numb," she called down to him. "I don't know how much longer I can hold on."

"Long enough," he yelled back. "You can hang on long enough to get back down here. I'll take it from there."

Joe went over the possibilities in his mind. He could have her start swinging her body toward the deck railing as soon as she got near enough. That way, he'd have several chances to grab her. He was bound to make good on one of them. But what if she didn't have the strength left to do her part?

He could wait until she was right in front of him, less than a couple of feet away. Then he could reach out, grab her under her arms, and hoist her inside the railing. But he'd have only one shot.

He could reach out for her legs as soon she came close enough, then, holding tight, fling her back across his shoulder like a large sack. But if she fell backward when he grabbed her instead of forward toward his shoulder, he could be pulled off balance and they would both crash to the ground.

None of the plans was perfect. Even worse, they all depended on Deb's trusting him enough to let go of the sail. Joe decided to try all three. One of them has to work, he told himself.

He tried to picture how the rescue would work.

As Deb approached, he'd ask her to swing toward him so he could catch her. If she didn't have the strength for that, he'd try to grab her legs and swing her over his shoulder. If that didn't work, he'd grab her under the arms when she was directly in front of him. And if that failed, he'd have one more chance to grab her legs as she started back up again.

"I'm slipping," Deb called, her voice shaky. Her anxious call brought him back to the present. "Here I come," she said. "Are you ready?"

"Absolutely," Joe answered. Deb's sail was horizontal and she dangled dangerously from the end. "I'm going to get you off there, Deb. Just do what I say, okay?"

"Whatever it takes," she said. She sounded determined. "Tell me what to do."

"When I give the word, you swing toward me. Give it everything you've got. I know you're tired, but try hard. We're almost there now." In spite of the adrenaline barreling through him, he managed a half smile in her direction.

As the sail carrying Deb grew nearer, Joe got ready. He planted his feet solidly on the deck and leaned against the railing for extra support. He watched for the perfect moment, then his voice exploded. "Now!" he yelled. "Swing toward me."

"Mmmmmmumph." Her breath came out in a whoosh. Still clinging tightly to the sail, she swung her body toward the railing. Joe reached out for her but grabbed only air.

"Again!" he yelled. "Now!" As Deb swung in, Joe reached out. With perfect timing, he caught her around the hips and held tightly. He felt the pull of the sail as it continued to move, still holding its cargo.

"Let go, Deb," Joe said, bracing himself. "Let go of the sail. I've got you."

With a "Yiiieee," Deb released her grip. The shift in momentum yanked Joe forward. But he was prepared. With a surge of strength, he pulled back, stumbling a little. He kept his balance and dropped Deb gently to her feet.

"Man, that was some ride," Joe said, smiling. Deb looked pale and shaky but otherwise okay.

"I don't recommend it," she said, her voice low. "Thanks," she said, flexing her fingers. "You saved my life—from the windmill and from the creep who forced me here in the first place."

"No problem," Joe said. "What happened exactly?"

"I got a call at the shop from someone who said he had information for Cody about Mike Brando. I was to tell Cody to meet this guy alone at the Polo Field."

"So did you?"

"Well, you know what Cody's been through over the last couple of days," Deb said with a small smile. "I figured he's just going to give him some information. Where's the danger?"

"So you decided to meet him yourself," Joe concluded. "I'm sure you didn't even mention it to Cody."

"You're right," Deb said, nodding.

"But how did you end up here?" Joe asked.

"I took a cab to the Polo Field and walked to the spot where we were to meet," Deb explained. "Someone came up behind me, stuck a gun in my back, and told me to walk to the parking lot."

"Did you see the gun?" Joe asked.

"Not really," Deb said, "but I felt something, and I didn't want to argue about it."

"Smart move, actually," Joe agreed. "Did you recognize the person's voice?"

"Not really," she said. "He talked in muffled grunts—didn't say much."

"How did you get to Cody's car?"

"It was weird," she said. "We were headed toward the parking lot when I spotted Cody's car. The guy told me to stop. I was really surprised to see Cody's car, so I was looking around for him. I don't know, maybe the guy was, too."

66

Joe remembered walking around the stands, trying to find the driver of the green car. "I must have been nearby," he said, "but I never saw you."

"Anyway," Deb continued, "he walked me over to Cody's car and ordered me to get in the backseat and put my head between my knees."

"I saw him pull away, but I didn't see you. No wonder," Joe said.

"He took me into the windmill and was going to tie me up, but I broke away. He was in front of the door, so I ran up the ladder to the deck. I figured I could yell for help, but he was right behind me."

"That must have been when I came in," Joe concluded.

"Yeah—you know the rest."

Joe pulled the cap he'd found out of his back pocket. "Was the man wearing this?"

"Not when I saw him, he wasn't," Deb answered. "I never saw him, really, until he came out on the deck. He was always behind me at the Polo Field. And it was so dark inside the windmill." She shuddered. "Let's get out of here."

In a few minutes they were out of the windmill and back in the garden. Deb looked up at the sails and shuddered again. "Wow," she whispered.

"There's Cody's car!" Deb exclaimed. She looked

across the drive as Joe followed her out of the windmill. "And a horse?"

"It's a long story," Joe said. "Are you really okay? Can you drive Cody's car back to the stables? I'll take the horse and meet you there."

"Sure," Deb answered. Joe handed her the keys. As she pulled out on to the street, he mounted the horse and followed.

When they got back to the stables, Joe returned the horse. Then he took the wheel of Cody's car. "Before we go, I'd like to check on something," he said, pulling away.

Joe drove back to the spot where the green car had been parked. "It's still there," he said when he spotted it. "I'm pretty sure that's the car your kidnapper abandoned to steal Cody's."

The green car was locked, but Joe could see from the papers lying on the front seat that it was a rental car. He wrote down the name and phone number of the car rental agency and a description of the car, including the license plate number.

Finally he and Deb left Golden Gate Park, and Joe drove them back to Skin & Bones. In his mind, he was going over his encounter with Deb's kidnapper, making sure he remembered every detail. "I haven't had any lunch," he finally said, "and it's nearly four o'clock. Let's pick up some food." They stopped for burgers and fries—enough for everybody.

Cody greeted them when they arrived and turned the Skin & Bones customers over to his salesclerk. "Let's go," he said to Joe and Deb. "Frank's upstairs. Wait till you hear what happened to us."

"Looks like we're going to have some major show-and-tell," Joe said. They joined Frank, who was sitting at the kitchen table, resting his bandaged ankle on a chair. "We've got our own tale," Joe added, "one we need to tell the police."

Frank raised his eyebrows at Cody. "Okay," Cody said with a resigned sigh. "I guess it's time to let Dad in on all this. Let's call him."

Deb reported her kidnapping to Sergeant Chang. Then Joe talked to Cody's dad, telling him that he thought the driver of the green car had followed them from his house. He also reported that Cody's car was stolen near where the green car was parked. But he agreed with Sergeant Chang there was no proof the driver of the green car stole the SUV.

"You'll need to speak to the police and give a description to the police artist," Joe said to Deb when he hung up. "They're sending a cruiser for you now."

"Okay," she responded. "But then I'm going home to bed. Today was way more excitement than I needed. Joe, you fill them in. I'll talk to you all later." Cody walked her to the door and waited with her until the cruiser arrived.

"Man, these smell good," Frank said, grabbing a burger. "Cody was just talking about going out to pick something up. We missed lunch."

"You, too?" Joe said. He reached for some fries, brushing a fly away from the bag. "Okay, you heard most of our story—all but the fun part about Deb and the windmill. I'll tell you about that in a minute. First, what happened to your ankle?" he asked Frank.

Frank told Joe about his encounter with Mike Brando. Cody came back and chimed in with a few angry additions.

"Whoa, that was close," Joe said when they'd finished. "It's a pretty big coincidence—you getting pushed out of the cable car and Brando appearing a few minutes later." He batted at another fly buzzing around his head. "Is there a door open somewhere?"

"Must be," Frank said, swatting at his own fly. "We seem to be sharing our meal with unexpected guests."

"No!" Cody yelled suddenly. He sprang up from his chair so fast that it fell over behind him.

Joe looked at Cody, then at Frank. Then he more closely studied the three small bugs crawling across the kitchen table. When he moved his hand, the bugs took to the air, joining a few others circling the counter.

Joe leaped up from his chair and headed for the stairs. Frank and Cody followed close behind. As they sprinted up to the lab, they were greeted by small swarms of flying insects.

The lab door was ajar. Joe pushed it open to see what looked like a scene from a horror movie.

The door to Bug Central stood open. Swarms of dermestid beetles darted from spot to spot, looking for leftover flesh on the bones and skins that were Cody's current lab projects. Uneven lines of small hairy caterpillars looped across the floor, inched up table legs, and hung from bookshelves.

8 The Clue in the Claw

There were bugs crawling and swarming everywhere.

"I'll get the door," Frank said.

"Yeah, close it. We can contain as many as possible in here for now. But it's really too late," Cody said sadly. "I'll have to call the fumigator. All my colonies are lost."

They left the lab, closing the door behind them. Cody went to the first floor to send the salesclerk home and close up the shop. Then he went back to his office to call the fumigator. Frank and Joe checked the doors and windows for signs of a break-in. The back door of the office looked as if it had been jimmied.

"Guys, you have to help me out," Cody said when he came back to the kitchen. "I have to stay here until

72

the fumigator arrives. But I told Jennifer Payton I'd bring over the stuff for her haunted house today. Can you take it over for me? You've got to get out of here, anyway."

He ran his fingers through his hair. "Dad's car is fixed, and he had the van delivered for you. I saw it parked around the corner. Just take it whenever you want. I'm going to have to stick around here until the fumigator's finished gassing the place. I'll call you later at Dad's."

"Is this going to be some sort of plague unleashed on the city of San Francisco?" Joe asked.

"No, actually dermestid beetles are common in households all over North America," Cody said. "Just not in concentrated colonies in such large numbers. People aren't aware of them because they're so small. But now that mine have busted out of Bug Central, I've got to get them cleaned out. If I don't, they'll ruin my clothes, furniture, everything."

"They didn't just bust out," Joe said.

"No, they didn't," Cody said through clenched teeth. "Someone let them out."

"We were all at your dad's last night and didn't get back here till this afternoon," Frank pointed out. "Plenty of time to do the damage here."

73

"If Mike Brando was driving that green car this morning, it means he knew we were at Dad's," Cody said. "He could have known we were there last night, too, and broken in here then. He knew all about the bugs. I'd shown them to him when he was my broker."

Cody showed the Hardys a stack of boxes. Inside were the bones and other spooky specimens he had set aside to lend to Jennifer for her haunted house. "Thanks for taking these over," he said, his voice low. "See you later. Don't tell Dad about the bugs. I want to tell him myself."

"Before we go, I want to get this key thing figured out," Joe said. "Whoever stole your car had a key, Cody. How many sets of keys to your SUV?"

"My regular set, which was in the car when you took it over, Joe," Cody answered. "And an extra set in my file cabinet."

"Maybe they're there," Frank said, "maybe not."

Cody raced to the file cabinet and pulled open the second drawer. After rummaging noisily around the file folders, he turned back to face the others.

"They're gone," he said, his face drawn into a tight scowl. "Whoever trashed my office Monday night must have pocketed them!"

Joe opened the owner's manual and showed

Cody the small brass chain. "Do these look familiar?"

"Yeah, that's them," Cody said.

"We'll give them to your dad," Frank said. "Maybe he can get some prints off them."

"Didn't you say the driver wore gloves?" Cody asked.

"Yes," Joe said. "But you never know. He—or she—might have touched them sometime with bare fingers. It won't hurt to run a test." He slipped the owner's manual back into his jacket pocket.

"Okay, let's go," Frank said. He and Joe piled the boxes on a couple of dollies.

"Cody's really down," Frank said as they worked. "Losing the beetle colony is a pretty low blow. We've got to find out who's doing this. His business can't stand much more trouble."

When they got outside, Joe stopped Frank for a minute to talk. They sat on a bench outside Skin & Bones. "Hey, Frank, are you sure you're okay?" Joe asked, looking at Frank's ankle. "Maybe *you* should see a doctor."

"I'm fine," Frank said. "It's just a little sore. And it looks like Mike Brando moves to the top of our suspect list—with at least one accomplice. Remember—if he's behind the attacks on Cody, he had to have an accomplice while he was in prison."

"And you and I were attacked in separate areas of the city at the same time by two different people," Joe said.

"That means we've also been branded as targets," Frank said.

Joe showed Frank the ski cap he had found in the windmill and the small cardboard disk that had fallen out of it.

"That looks familiar," Frank said. "Cody had a disk like that in his desk drawer, but it had a different number printed across the center."

"What is it?" Joe asked.

"It's a tag for a locker at his mailing station. He gets so many weird packages—some of them really large—so he has many of them delivered to a mailing station over on Larkin. They rent him a refrigerated locker there. The number on the front of the tag is the locker number; the number on the back is the combination to the locker padlock."

"Good," Joe said. "Something else to check. We're finally getting somewhere."

"First, let's get this stuff next door," Frank said. "Jennifer's waiting for it."

"Before we leave, I want to take another look around Cody's roof," Joe said as they pushed the dollies up the sidewalk. "I didn't get enough time to do a good search. I'd like to have a little more to go on than that scrap of mirror."

Frank and Joe took the Skin & Bones merchandise into Reflections. Then Joe excused himself so he could pay a return visit to Cody's roof while it was still light.

Meanwhile, Jennifer took Frank on a quick tour of the club. The ceiling of the large room was draped in black, with occasional bursts of tiny red twinkle lights. The large room was divided into small cubicles.

"Each cubicle will have a separate scary scene," Jennifer explained.

"This is quite a place," Frank said.

"I inherited it from my grandmother about a year ago," Jennifer said. "What you see is just the beginning. I'm expanding it big-time. I want to add a restaurant, an outdoor café . . . maybe a small theater. I'd like to see this neighborhood move from basically retail shops to more of an entertainment area. You know . . . theaters, music and comedy clubs, restaurants."

Jennifer piled costumes on to Frank's outstretched arms. "I need to take care of some things," she announced. "Here are the outfits for all of you. We've got a short dress rehearsal Thursday evening and a party for all the volunteers afterward. Will you and the others come early and help me set up?"

"That'd be fun," Frank said. "See you then. Before I go, may I use your phone?"

"Sure," Jennifer said. "There's one in my office in the far corner.

Frank sat behind Jennifer's desk and checked the phone number for the mailing station Cody had mentioned. He dialed the number, and while he waited, he looked at the display of photographs on Jennifer's wall. She's a sports and fitness fanatic, he thought to himself. There were photos of Jennifer dressed in every conceivable sports uniform and receiving certificates and awards for every conceivable competition.

The taped recording told him that the mail stations were closed until seven o'clock the next morning. The room with private mailboxes and lockers was open twenty-four hours.

Joe was walking in as Frank was walking out. "Did you find anything?" Frank asked his brother as they got into Sergeant Chang's van.

"No," Joe said. "Nothing."

On the way back to Sergeant Chang's, Frank and Joe continued to compare notes. "I know I was pushed off that cable car," Frank said. "I can't prove it—but I felt two strong hands on my back."

"It can't be just a coincidence that Mike Brando was nearby," Joe pointed out.

"I might not have been the target," Frank said. "He could have been following Cody and meant to push him. Just when he started to shove, he could have been jostled, lost his balance, and I was the one in the street."

"How about the guy on the windmill deck?" Frank asked. "We're pretty sure it's the same guy who was driving the green car, right?"

"Seems likely," Joe agreed. "The car was parked right there."

"Could it be the same guy who kicked you on the roof?"

"I didn't get much of an idea about the one on the roof," Joe reminded him. "First he was crouching, then I was bent over, then he was gone. Actually, it's pretty much the same thing with the guy on the windmill deck. His back was to me most of the time. Then when he turned around, I was distracted by the danger facing Deb."

Frank told Joe about calling the mailing station. "We should get on that," he said. "That could lead to something."

79

"So how does the club look?" Joe asked. "Is it going to be pretty scary?"

"It's going to be cool. The kids should love it." Frank told Joe about Jennifer's plans for the neighborhood.

"Does Cody know about this?"

"He hasn't mentioned anything to me," Frank said.

"It doesn't sound like his shop will fit the image she has in mind."

The house was empty when they arrived at Sergeant Chang's. He had left them a note saying he wouldn't be home until later and to help themselves to anything in the kitchen. He also mentioned that a package had been left for them.

The bulky bundle lay on the table next to the note. It was wrapped in brown paper and tied with strong cord. There was no return name or address—just the delivery service stamp and the word *Hardys* typed on a small label taped to the brown paper.

Frank cut the string and pulled back the paper. Inside lay a deep wooden box with a sliding lid. Carefully, Frank slid the top of the box to one end and lifted it out of the groove. Pale yellow tissue paper concealed a lumpy package. Cautiously, Frank peeled the tissue off a gruesome sight.

"Whoa, it's some kind of a claw!" Joe said, his voice

hushed. An animal foot covered with long black hair lay on the paper. Projecting out from the top were very long gray nails which hooked around and under the hairy claw.

Joe pulled a piece of paper from under the claw. The message was neatly typed from a computer printer: "Stop following me or the next package of bones might be yours."

9 A Bloody Visit

Cautiously, using the tissue paper as a shield, Frank picked the hairy claw up out of the deep wooden box and examined it. There were no tags or identifying labels attached to the grisly object.

"I'm calling Cody," Joe said, reaching for the phone. Cody picked up after the first ring.

Joe quickly told Cody about the package.

"It's an anteater claw," Cody said, his voice sounding as if his jaw were clamped shut. Joe could tell he was furious. "Probably the one from the zoo packages that were stolen from me!"

"Here's something," Frank called to Joe. Carefully, he pulled back the hair from the underside of the claw. A tattoo marked the skin beneath the hair. "Ask

Cody if this means anything," Frank said. Then he read the tattoo. "X-3-7-C2."

Joe repeated the tattooed numbers to Cody.

"Just a second," Cody said through the phone receiver. "Let me check my order sheet."

Joe could hear paper rustling, and then Cody returned to the phone. "Yes," Cody said. "That's one of the anteater claws I picked up Monday. But how come he sent it to *you* and not me?"

"Don't forget, the driver of the green car followed us from your dad's," Joe pointed out. "So he's probably been staking the place out. He must know we're staying here and we're friends of yours."

"Mike Brando knows who my father is," Cody offered. "He could definitely be behind all this."

"Is he wondering why we got the package?" Frank asked. Joe nodded.

"Somebody's obviously been staking out your place, too," Frank called out, loud enough for Cody to hear. "He or she could have seen us coming and going. If the driver of the green car sent the package, it could be a warning after his run-in with Joe this afternoon."

"Man, we've got to get this guy," Cody said in Joe's ear.

"How are the beetles?" Joe asked. "Did the fumigator come yet?"

"The beetles are making their way from Bug Central to Bug Heaven," Cody said. "Did you get things set up with Jennifer okay?"

"Yes, we did," Joe answered. "How well do you know her?"

"Not at all," Cody said. "We just met the other day."

"Did you hear about her expansion plans?" Joe asked. "How she wants to change this neighborhood from retail to entertainment."

"No," Cody said. "What do you mean?"

Joe repeated what Jennifer had said. "She really wants to change the atmosphere of the neighborhood."

"I haven't heard a thing about it." Cody's voice got a little louder. "And speaking as a retailer, I'm not sure I like it."

Then Cody switched subjects. "Is Dad there?" he asked.

"Not yet," Joe answered. "He left us a note saying he'd be back later."

"Well, Dave called," Cody said. "We were supposed to meet him for dinner tonight, remember? I told him about the bugs. I'm going to meet him at Dad's in about an hour. I'll just pick up something for us to eat. I don't feel much like going out."

"Okay, great," Joe said. "See you soon."

After Joe hung up, he and Frank wrapped the

anteater claw back in the yellow tissue paper. Then Joe set it down in the shredded plastic foam it had been packed in. Frank fit the wooden lid into its groove, slid it closed, and put the box on the kitchen counter. Then he and Joe went to their room to clean up.

Frank showered first. He pulled on jeans and a blue sweater. Then, while Joe took his turn in the shower, Frank turned on Sergeant Chang's computer and searched the Internet for the mailing station company. He wanted to track down the locker that matched the disk Joe had found in the windmill.

"Yes," he said aloud, when he found that the company had a website. There was information about the company's services, branch offices and addresses, and other contact information.

The company had several branches, and each specialized in a specific type of mailing or storage facility. There was only one branch that featured large refrigerated lockers—the one where Cody had his account.

The website also featured layouts of each branch, showing different sizes of lockers and mailboxes. Each box and locker was numbered. Number 5773 was a large refrigerated box in the same branch as Cody's.

Then Frank called the courier service that had delivered the strange package.

"Listen to this," Frank reported when Joe emerged from the shower. "I just talked to the delivery service that brought us the anteater claw. It's an outfit that specializes in offbeat deliveries."

"I think ours certainly qualifies," Joe said. He pulled on jeans and a Forty-niners sweatshirt.

"They advertise that they will deliver anything, anywhere, anytime. The girl I talked to said they get a lot of unusual jobs. She took the order for our package by phone."

"No name, I'm sure," Joe said.

"Right."

"Could she tell if it was a man or a woman?" Joe asked.

"She thought it was a man, but she wasn't sure. No one ever saw the person who ordered the delivery. The weird part is where they had to pick up the package."

"Where?" Joe said.

"Muir Woods," Frank announced.

"The redwood forest? North of the city?" Joe asked.

"That's what the courier said," Frank answered. "He was directed to a hollow tree in a secluded area of the forest. The package was in there, along with an envelope of cash to pay for the delivery."

"No check, no credit card," Joe observed. "Nothing to trace back to the sender."

Frank grabbed the keys to the van and his beat-up leather jacket. "I'm going to the delivery service office. They're open twenty-four hours. The girl says the courier who brought us the claw is on a run right now, but should be back in about fifteen minutes."

"Okay, I'll stay here. Cody should be here soon—I'll try to save some food for you." Joe gave his brother a big grin.

While Joe was combing his hair, he thought he heard a sound in the driveway.

"Cody?" Joe called. "Sergeant Chang?"

Then it was quiet. He heard nothing.

Then another noise caught his attention. It was like a scraping or a scuffling outside.

"Is that you, Frank?" Joe called. "I'm just about—"

Joe's words were cut off by a thunderous pounding on the front door. It felt as if the whole house was vibrating.

"Boy, somebody definitely wants in," Joe said in a low voice, "or we're having one of San Francisco's famous earthquakes."

The pounding stopped and it was very quiet.

Joe moved soundlessly to the front door, every nerve alive and alert.

He looked through the peephole but saw nothing.

Slowly, he inched open the front door. A cool wash of foggy evening air sent a chill through him.

At first he saw nothing. Then from beside the door, a man took one step toward him and fell into Joe without a word. "Cody," the man whispered as he slid to the floor, his jacket smeared with streaks of blood.

10 Two Heads Are Better

Dave Cloud fell against Joe, who tried to catch him, but Dave slipped from his grasp and slumped to the floor. Joe's sweatshirt was streaked with blood where Dave had fallen against him.

Joe knelt next to Dave and took his wrist.

"What happened?" Frank asked, running up the front walk.

"It's Dave," Joe said. "His pulse seems okay."

Dave's head rolled from side to side, and his eyes opened. "Hey, Joe," he mumbled. "What's up?"

Dave sat up and took a deep breath, but before he could say anything, Cody burst up the front walk, too, his arms full of sacks.

Frank and Joe were helping Dave stand. "It's not as

89

bad as it looks," Dave said, brushing at his blood-stained jacket.

Cody put down the bags of food and helped the Hardys get Dave into the house and into a chair. "Here. Sit," he ordered Dave.

"Really, I'm not hurt that bad," Dave said with a slight smile. While he peeled off his jacket, his expression turned to anger. "It was Brando."

"Man, that guy is really getting around," Joe said.

"Look," Frank interrupted. "While you're talking, I'm going to take you to the hospital. You could be seriously injured."

Frank stood up and started toward Dave, but Dave stopped him. "Nah, I don't think so," he said. "I'll be okay. I'll get cleaned up and you'll see. It looks a lot worse than it is."

Dave rolled up his shirtsleeve to reveal a cut on his forearm. While he washed his wound in the bathroom, Dave told the others what had happened.

"I was getting ready to come over here," he began. "I thought I heard a noise outside my apartment, but I checked and didn't see anyone. I made a couple of calls, then left. Someone jumped me as I walked to the car."

"And you're sure it was Mike Brando?" Frank asked.

Dave had a small cut on his chin. He dabbed it with

an ice cube to stop the bleeding. "It was dark," he finally answered. "So I didn't get a good look at his face, but I'm sure it was Brando."

"Why?" Joe asked.

"His voice," Dave answered. "I'd know that sound anywhere."

Frank flashed back on his encounter with Brando. Dave was right. Brando's voice was different. It was deep and rumbly, like a wildcat's growl.

"What did he say?" Joe asked.

"Not much that made sense," Dave replied. He dried his hands and dropped the towel on the counter. "He mumbled something about payback and settling scores with old enemies. Oh, and he mentioned your name, Cody."

"Yeah?" Cody said. "Sent me his best wishes, I'll bet."

"Not exactly." Dave gave Cody a crooked smile. "He said to tell you that Skin and Bones is going down—and you and I are going with it. He's angry with me because I was your partner when he was caught."

"Sorry about that," Cody said. "You had nothing to do with Brando's troubles."

"Well, you've heard the old saying about the company you keep," Dave said with a weak smile. "Just kidding, of course. He still associates me with the business, I guess."

Cody handed Dave some antiseptic lotion.

"How'd you get that cut?" Frank asked. Dave's arm had stopped bleeding, but it was swollen and looked sore.

"Brando had a knife," Dave said. "He came right at me with it. I was able to deflect the blow, but he swiped my arm." Wincing, Dave dabbed some of the antiseptic on the cut, and Cody and Frank bandaged Dave's arm.

"Did you report your attack to the police?" Frank asked.

"Sure," Dave said. "I stopped at a station on my way over here. I was okay then, but by the time I got here, I was pretty shaky."

"You lost a lot of blood," Joe said, looking at Dave's jeans and shirt. "Your clothes are a mess."

"Come on," Cody said to Dave. "I'll get you some clean clothes. I've still got stuff here in my old room."

"No, I'm going home," Dave said. "This shook me pretty good. I'll talk to you later."

While Joe changed his blood-smeared sweatshirt for a sweater, Frank and Cody laid out their meal in the dining room—a feast of Mexican favorites.

The three eagerly dug into their dinner. "What a day," Joe said. "I am so hungry."

"What about tomorrow?" Cody asked. "I'm going to

have to stay here again tonight. In fact, I have to close the shop for twenty-four hours. The smell's pretty gross. So I'm available to help you dig into my case."

"We finally have some real leads," Frank said. He told Cody about what he'd learned from the delivery service. "In fact, that's where I was before Dave got here."

"Did the courier have any more information to offer?" Joe asked.

Frank reached into his pocket and pulled out a piece of paper. "I say we check this out," he said.

He laid the paper on the table. It was a rough-drawn map in an area of Muir Woods. He pointed to an X at the top. "I had the courier draw it for me. This is the tree where he picked up the anteater claw."

"Yeah, I sort of know where that is," Cody said. "I mountain bike up in that area." He hoisted himself up to sit on the counter.

"But isn't Muir Woods a public park?" Joe asked. "Wouldn't somebody see the package and rip it off?"

"There are regular trails," Cody said. "But there are some very secluded areas in the fringes of the forest, off the public trails. You're not supposed to go there, of course. Most people don't. But if you really know your way around, you could probably pull it off."

Frank could see that Cody was excited about the

prospect. "It's so dark in there," Cody added, "even during the daytime. The trees are enormous and block out most of the sunshine. It's still very primitive and wild. There's no real development except for the visitors' center and a few marked trails."

"We'll go tomorrow," Frank said.

"Sounds like a plan," Joe agreed.

"I've got more information," Frank said. "While I was out, I stopped at the mailing station. The private boxes and lockers are open twenty-four hours a day.

"And?" Cody urged.

"The good news is that I found the locker that matches the tag Joe found," Frank said.

"Did the combination work?" Joe asked.

"It did," Frank answered, taking a gulp from his soda.

Then Cody turned to Frank. "So what's the bad news?" he asked.

"There was nothing in the locker but a few scraps of brown paper," Frank said, dropping the fragments on the table.

Joe turned a couple of them over. They were blank on both sides. "No clues here," he agreed.

"I did get a look at the locker register," Frank said, "while the night clerk was busy on a personal phone call. There was no name matched to my locker—only the code b-two-g."

They all thought about what Frank had said. Finally Joe stood up. "I'm going for ice cubes," he said. "Speak now if you want anything."

Joe went to the kitchen. As he walked toward the refrigerator, a movement in the driveway caught his attention.

He walked to the back door and stared out the window. But he could see nothing but the shadowy forms of Sergeant Chang's trimmed hedges and bushes. As he turned toward the refrigerator, a faint noise outside pulled him back to the door.

Joe turned the doorknob on the back door slowly, so it wouldn't make any noise. Behind him he could hear Frank and Cody planning the Muir Woods excursion for the next day.

He stepped out into the cool night and moved toward the direction of the sound he'd heard. It was quiet now, except for the noisy yakking of a Steller's jay high in a eucalyptus tree.

Without making a sound, Joe crept toward the red van. He walked around the drive but saw and heard nothing. He opened the van and put one knee on the driver's seat, so he could lean in and look into the back. It all looked the same as when he and Frank had returned here.

He swung around and sat in the driver's seat. He

checked the visor and the dash. Then he reached for the glove compartment. As he did, a movement on the floor in front of the passenger seat caught the corner of his eye.

Joe froze. Holding his breath, he looked down. Coiled on the floor in a pretzel-like pile beneath his arm was a large, dark, thick snake. Its flat, blunt head rose up out of the pile and began a slow but threatening dance.

11 Another Suspect?

Don't move, Joe told himself. Don't even breathe. His eyes narrowed as he focused on the coil and the thick clublike end that wove its threats in the air.

As his gaze intensified, Joe made a startling discovery. This snake's head had no eyes, no mouth! Joe's breathing started to return in small sips. That's the tail, he realized. This snake is waving its tail!

Joe knew he still had to get his arm out of the way—and the sooner the better. With a gasp Joe raised his arm straight up until it hit the top of the van.

The snake convulsed along its whole coil, then disappeared beneath the passenger seat.

Joe was out of the van in an instant, locking the door behind him. As he raced up the sidewalk to the house, one of the shadowy forms that looked just like another bush began to run.

Joe changed directions immediately and angled off in pursuit. He ran the man down half a block away. With one giant dive, he hurled himself at the running figure, bringing the person down with a crunching thud.

"Aaaahhhh," the man yelled as Joe decked him. It was a strange, low, throaty rumble.

"You must be Mike Brando," Joe said, pinning the man's arms behind him. "I've been hearing a lot about you the last couple of days. You seem to be living up to your reputation."

With his free hand, Joe patted Brando down. "Well, look at this," Joe said, pulling a small revolver out of Brando's boot. "Another parole violation. Okay, come on." He pulled Brando up.

"Let go of me," Brando growled. "You don't have the right to hold me." He seemed to want to struggle, but Joe's slamming blow had apparently knocked the wind out of him.

"Well, let's just go back to the house and check that out with Sergeant Chang, shall we?" Joe said. Still holding Brando's wrists behind him, Joe pushed the man across the lawn and in the back door of Sergeant Chang's house.

"You asked us if we wanted you to bring us anything," Frank said with a surprised smile when Joe shoved Brando into the kitchen. "We didn't think to ask for Mike Brando." He went to the phone and called nine-one-one while Joe tied Brando to a chair with a rope he found in the cleaning closet.

"Brando!" Cody said, joining Frank in the kitchen. "Finally, we'll put an end to your sabotage and dirty tricks."

"You think this is the end of it?" Brando snarled. "It's just the beginning. Putting me away isn't going to stop me," he continued.

"Because you have help on the outside?" Frank suggested. "Was someone working with you while you were in prison?"

"And was it the same person attacking Deb and Joe in Golden Gate Park while you were stalking us on the cable car?" Cody added. "And what about stabbing Dave Cloud just a few hours ago? How long did it take you to plan all this, Mike?"

"What are you talking about?" Brando grumbled. "I don't know anything about anything in Golden Gate Park."

"That's okay," Joe said. "You don't have to tell us, but the police will have to hear about it."

Brando's chin jutted out as he glared at Cody.

"And how about the little present in the van," Joe said. "Don't tell us you don't know anything about that."

Brando's face broke out in a nasty grin. "The snake I'll admit to," he said.

"Snake!" Cody said. Joe told Frank and Cody about his encounter in the van.

"Sounds like a rubber boa," Cody said. "They're called the two-headed snake because both ends look alike. A rubber boa likes to stay hidden, but when it feels threatened, it winds up into a tight ball. Then it raises its tail up and waves it as if it's about to strike with it. They're pretty common around here because they like to hang out in forests."

"Just a little tidbit for your collection, Chang," Brando said. "Not quite dead yet, of course, but all things in time. Those crazy bugs of yours will make short work of it."

"My beetles," Cody said, heading for Brando, his fists clenched. "You ruined my colonies."

"Easy, Cody," Frank said. "We've got him now. He'll be going back to prison for sure."

"Yeah?" Brando barked. "Well, they can't keep me in there forever. I'll get out again. And when I do, you'd better be ready."

"You might be in a little longer this time," Joe

pointed out. "Attacking me with a snake and pushing my brother off a moving cable car could be interpreted as attempted murder."

"The cable car wasn't moving," Brando said, raising his voice. "And I wasn't after your brother, anyway," he added. "Somebody bumped me. I meant to push you—it should have been you!" He tried to jump at Cody, but the rope Joe had tied held him fast to the chair.

"So you did do it," Joe said, smiling at Cody. "You did push Frank."

Brando flashed a mean look at Joe, then sank into surly silence.

"Dad!" Cody called, looking gratefully toward the door as his father walked in with two uniformed officers.

"I picked up on the nine-one-one call," Sergeant Chang said. "Everybody okay?" He looked from Cody to Frank to Joe. They all nodded back to him.

"There's a rubber boa in the van," Cody said.

"Well, Mike, here we are again," Sergeant Chang said, shaking his head. "I thought you were headed for a quieter life up north."

"No lectures, Chang," Brando said. "Just get me out of here so I can talk to my attorney in private."

"You take him to the station and the snake to Animal Control," Sergeant Chang told the officers. "I'll get the statements here and meet you there shortly."

Sergeant Chang took out his pen and notebook. "Now, what happened here?" he asked his son as Brando was led away.

"Joe can tell you," Cody said. "He's the one who got him. Frank and I haven't even heard what happened yet."

Joe filled them in on his encounter in the backyard. Then Cody told him about the disaster at Bug Central.

Breathing a long "Wheeeeeew," Sergeant Chang leaned back in his chair. "You boys have been pretty busy, haven't you?" he said with a big grin.

Then he leaned forward again, and his manner and voice were serious. "Okay, guys, now it's time to turn the case over to the police. We'll put Brando back where he belongs and track down his accomplices, if any. You have done a great job, but there have been too many close calls."

Sergeant Chang stood up and put his notebook back in his pocket. "Joe, you might need to come to the station and go over your complaint again. Until then, I know it'll be hard, but you and Frank try to remember you're on vacation—not on assignment. If anything happened to you here in my city, your father would never forgive me. Cody, you leave Mike

Brando to me. I'm going to see how the questioning is going. I'll keep you all posted.".

Sergeant Chang left and Frank, Joe, and Cody sank into comfortable chairs with fresh cans of soda.

"Okay, so we still go to Muir Woods tomorrow, right?" Cody asked.

"Absolutely," Joe said. "It's not possible for Brando to have done everything that's happened since we've been here—let alone all the things that have happened to you, Cody."

"Right," Frank said. "Either he has someone working with him, or we've got more than one culprit. The field trip tomorrow is still on."

"And don't forget," Joe reminded them. "We have to be back by late afternoon to help Jennifer Payton set up the haunted house for the dress rehearsal."

"Yikes!" Cody said. "I forgot about that."

"No problem," Frank said. "We'll get an early start. My tour book says Muir Woods opens at eight in the morning."

"Too early," Cody said, shaking his head. "We don't need to go that early."

A ringing phone interrupted him. Cody answered it, spoke for a few minutes, and then hung up.

"That was Dad," he said, walking back into the kitchen. He carried a small pile of mail. "Brando's in major trouble. Attacking you two plus breaking so many parole violations—he's not going to be out for quite a while."

"Did he give them any clues about accomplices?" Joe asked.

"He still says he didn't do any of the other stuff and doesn't know who did," Cody answered, "but they're going to keep questioning him. He'll break down eventually. They ran a check on the green car rental, but the name and the prints on the keys didn't bring anything up. Dad thinks the guy used a phony name and fake ID."

The Hardys and Cody agreed they deserved some serious sack time, so after going over the next day's plans one more time, they headed for their beds.

Thursday morning started with the usual fog, but the radio weather station predicted a sunnier afternoon.

Cody made a quick run over to Skin & Bones to make sure everything was okay after the fumigator's visit. Frank and Joe had breakfast and dressed in jeans, sweaters, and boots.

Cody arrived back in less than an hour. "Look who I found," he said. "She was at Skin and Bones picking up the mail. Since we can't work today anyway, I asked her if she wanted to go with us to the woods."

Deb walked in. She was carrying her briefcase, but was dressed in jeans, a white T-shirt, and a tan jacket. Her thick blond hair was caught up under a baseball cap.

"First you have to see the letter we got today," Deb said. She dug down into her briefcase. "You know, it's getting close to your anniversary date." She pulled out a long envelope. "Almost time to renew your lease for this building."

"So, what's the deal?" Cody asked. "They've raised the rent so much I can't afford to stay here any longer?"

"Actually, I don't know yet. We didn't receive the lease—just this letter."

Cody scanned the letter quickly. Frank watched as Cody's mouth dropped open. "What!" Cody said. "I don't believe it." He turned to Frank and Joe. "My building's been sold," he said. "And guess who the new owner is."

His dark eyes flashed from Joe to Frank. "It's Jennifer Payton."

12 The Skull in the Forest

"Jennifer Payton has bought my building," Cody said.

"And you didn't know anything about it?" Frank asked.

"This is a complete surprise," Cody answered. "She never said a word to me."

"She told me she's planning to expand her club," Frank said.

"Yeah, like maybe expand right into my building," Cody said. He slumped into his chair. "I'm just getting the business to a point where people know where I am, and then she buys the building and kicks me out."

"You don't suppose . . ." Deb started to say.

"Well, it is odd that she hasn't said anything to Cody

about it," Joe said. "And she's got some pretty big plans for that area."

"She told me that she's hoping to help convert this neighborhood from retail stores to an entertainment hub," Frank told Deb. "Clubs, restaurants, places like that."

"And she thinks Skin and Bones doesn't exactly fit that image, I suppose," Deb concluded.

"Could be," Frank said.

"What if maybe she thinks she can drive me out by messing with my business," Cody said. His words sounded clipped through his clenched jaw. "Maybe it's time to tell her just how wrong she is."

"Cool it," Frank said. "We're going to be there this afternoon. We can snoop around then—*and* in disguise."

"All right!" Cody said. "To the woods." He threw a couple of sweatshirts at the Hardys. "Here, take these," he said. "It can be really cool up there."

"Get your backpacks," Frank said to Joe and Cody. "We need to be prepared to bring back anything and keep our fingerprints off it. So we need flashlights, a couple of clean towels or rags, gloves, camera, army knife."

"How about tools," Joe added. "Cody, can we borrow one of your dad's screwdrivers and a small pair of pliers? You never know . . ."

"Do you have any brushes with you?" Deb asked Cody. "An archaeologist's brush—one of the ones you use to clean your specimens. You never know what you might find on the forest floor, and we may need to brush it off."

"Great idea, Deb," Frank said with a smile.

"No problem," Cody said. "I've plenty of them in my car. Deb, here's an extra backpack for you."

"Can we stop at a dry cleaner's?" Joe asked as they climbed into Cody's SUV. "This thing's a mess." He held up the sweatshirt he had been wearing when Dave fell against him. It was smeared with blood.

At the cleaner's he handed the stained sweatshirt to the clerk. The woman gave Joe an odd look when she saw it and acted as if she didn't even want to touch it. She carefully swept it into a bag, marked it for special treatment, and gave Joe a claim check.

Cody drove to the north end of the city and on to San Francisco's famous Golden Gate Bridge. They were headed north across the bay. Frank looked out the window. The dusky Pacific Ocean stretched out to the left. The sun topped off the waves with dazzling yellow light.

To the right, the water curved into San Francisco

Bay. Alcatraz Island sat in the middle, and from that distance, it almost looked like an oversize houseboat.

They reached the other side of the bridge and drove under the rainbow painted above the arch of the Marin Tunnel. Along the way Frank, Joe, and Cody told Deb about Dave's confrontation with Mike Brando, Frank's discovery in the mailing locker, and the boa that led to Joe's capture of Brando.

After a few miles Cody pulled off the main highway and on to the road leading to Muir Woods.

"Parts of the woods are really dense," Cody reminded them. "These are coastal redwoods, so they're huge. Some are two hundred fifty feet tall, and the trunks can be fourteen feet across."

"And they're old," Deb added. "The oldest tree in Muir Woods is one thousand years old. Most of the mature trees are between five hundred and eight hundred years old."

"Where will we be parking?" Frank asked.

"There's a parking area outside the entrance for visitors' cars and tour buses," Deb said.

"Let's not park in the lot," Frank suggested. "It might be better if Cody's car wasn't sitting empty in the parking area—just in case."

The two-lane road curled around deep canyons and up through Mount Tamalpais State Park. At times

Frank felt as if they were riding along the edge of the world.

Then they seemed to plunge into darkness as the road wound through a dark wilderness of trees and brush.

Finally Cody pulled off the road into a secluded grove of eucalyptus trees and parked the car. "We're a couple of miles from the Muir Woods entrance," he said. "I park here when I come up to mountain bike."

They all strapped on their backpacks. Cody and Frank pulled on sweatshirts. Joe and Deb tied theirs around their waists. Then they started up the road to Muir Woods.

It took them about half an hour to reach the park entrance. As they approached the visitor center, Frank felt a chill. Cody was right, he told himself. It is cooler in the redwoods.

They bought tickets and headed into the forest. "Take a look at this," Joe called to Frank. "It's amazing."

He stood next to an exhibit that was a slice of a tree trunk standing on its side like a wheel. The wood was divided into hundreds of rings. A chart showed how the rings helped define the age of the tree.

Frank was impatient to get moving, so he hustled the others on to the dirt path into the woods. The trees seemed to reach beyond their sight. When

Frank looked up, all he could see were hundreds of huge red-brown trunks. The branches with their green needles didn't start until way above them, and they seemed to form a far-off roof. He could just barely make out small patches of blue-white sky.

There was a group of young schoolchildren ahead on the main path. Otherwise, there were just a few visitors, scattered in twos and threes.

Occasionally they came across an enormous trunk that had fallen across the path. A small sign told them when the tree had fallen, how old it was, and that it would be left alone, as part of the natural evolution of the forest.

"This place is kind of spooky," Joe whispered. "I feel like I've gone back in time. Like I'm going to suddenly see a T. rex. Or a pterodactyl's going to make a surprise landing."

It was very quiet. The forest was so ancient, so mysterious, that everyone spoke in low voices.

Frank checked the map the courier had drawn for him. "It's up that way," he said, pointing. "That's where the delivery guy picked up the package with the anteater claw."

Frank led Joe, Deb, and Cody on to the upper path for a couple hundred yards. An older woman passed them going in the opposite direction. No one else was on their path.

Finally Frank stopped. "Okay, we have to leave the path here. Let's do it so no one sees us."

They glanced around. There was no one in sight. Quickly they stepped off the path through a dense carpet of ferns and into a very dark, secluded area of the forest.

At last they came to the tree that the courier had drawn on the map. "This has to be it," Frank whispered. "This is where the courier picked up the package."

Using their flashlights and sticks to brush away the undergrowth, they scanned the area for clues—anything that might lead them to the person who had sent the anteater claw.

But they found nothing. Joe looked up. The forest was so dense in this area that he could see only one tiny patch of sky. A gray-blue veil of fog twisted down through the opening. He could hear occasional crackling noises and faint swishes and scurries. A chill across his shoulders sent his body into a shudder. He untied the sweatshirt and pulled it over his head.

As he looked around, the huge tree trunks made him feel as if he were gazing into a funhouse mirror that had reduced his size.

Joe concentrated his gaze on the ground off to the right. It was different from the forest floor where they stood.

He took a few steps in that direction. The ferns were bent and lying flat on the ground. Fallen tree bark was splintered and smashed. Occasional spots of dirt were stomped. It looked almost as if someone had forged a crude path.

Joe hurried along, following the trail of trampled plants and redwood chips. His breath caught in his throat when he saw blurry impressions in the dirt that might have been footprints.

He moved faster, casting his flashlight beam ahead. Behind him, he heard the others begin to follow.

There was no sound in front of him. Not even the scampering and slithering noises he had heard before. Just the stillness of the forest.

His eyes fixed intently on the flashlight beam, which bounced ahead of him with every footfall. Then something jarred the continuous dark picture of dirt and ferns and chips of redwood bark.

Something very pale glinted at the left edge of the flashlight beam. Joe stopped suddenly and realized he'd been holding his breath. As he took in a gulp of air, he turned the flashlight. He aimed it to capture the ghostly vision.

A thin stream of fog wove in and out of the tree trunks, and it almost seemed to blur Joe's vision as he stared at the pale object. He squinted to get a clearer picture.

As the fog drifted away, Joe's breath caught again. Resting on rust-colored shards of bark was a human skull.

13 A Werewolf Warning

As Joe stared at the human skull, a large brown spider slithered out of one of the eye sockets.

"Looks like something out of the shop, Cody," Deb added, standing next to Joe.

"Let's take a look," Cody said, moving ahead.

"Wait!" Frank ordered. "It could be a kind of trap." He swung his flashlight around, but they saw nothing but tree trunks and ferns. "It's probably not a setup," Frank added. "But let's be careful, just in case."

"You three stay here and keep your lights burning," Joe said. "I'll check it out."

Cautiously, he moved toward the skull. He took each step very carefully, tapping the ground with his toe first, then setting down his whole foot. When he got to the skull, he prodded it—very gently—with a stick.

The skull rolled on to its side, and another spider skittered out between two teeth. Finally Joe knelt beside the skull and rolled it a couple of times with the stick. The others joined him then, kneeling on the redwood bark chips.

"I don't see any marks or tattoos on the skull," Cody said. "Of course, you can remove marks pretty easily from bone. Most bones have a few knicks and dings in them anyway, so shaving off a mark is no big deal." He carefully wrapped the skull in a rag and put it in his backpack.

"Do we know where we are?" Joe asked, looking around. "We've come pretty far off the park trail."

Frank got out the Muir Woods map and laid it next to the map drawn by the courier. "We're about here, I think," he concluded, pointing to the Muir Woods map.

"You're right on, Frank," Cody said. "In fact, we're not far from a trail that leads to the beach. Dad used to take me fishing down there."

"I want to keep going this way," Joe said. "Okay, it's not a path exactly, but someone's been through here—maybe someone who dropped the skull."

The trail led deeper into the forest about sixty yards, and then the air changed. The heavy dank

116

smell of wood and forest undergrowth gave way to the crisper air of ocean and fog.

Joe, Frank, Deb, and Cody followed the makeshift trail until they arrived at the edge of a bluff fringed with a wide stand of cypress trees. At last they could put away their flashlights. A steep path led down to a strip of beach.

"Hey, that's not my beach," Cody said, gazing down from the edge of the bluff. The ocean rolled in around several enormous rocks to a small strip of sand. The rocks served as a windbreak, protecting the small inlet.

"We've come this far," Joe said, "I'm not stopping now." He began the steep descent down the bluff. Frank, Deb, and Cody followed.

When they reached the bottom of the bluff, they came to a wire fence. "This probably means this is private property," Deb pointed out.

"Maybe," Joe said. "Maybe not."

"What's this?" Frank asked, stopping suddenly. He reached through the fence. Something had blown up against the other side and was stuck. It looked like a piece of fabric, about six inches square. But Frank was pretty sure it was something much more exotic.

"Cody, you have to see this," Deb said.

Gingerly Frank peeled the thin scrap off the wire

and pulled it through to his side of the fence. It was tan with a light pink pattern like patchwork. "Snakeskin?" he asked.

"It sure is," Cody said. "Probably an Argentine pink aboma," he added. "A pretty strange find out here."

"Why?" Joe asked.

"They're not native to California," Cody said.

"So how did it get here?" Frank wondered. "Come on, let's get closer." He was over the fence in seconds and walking toward a large rocky bluff.

The others followed quickly. They continued walking along the fence, but on the ocean side. As they neared the bluff, Frank stopped, gesturing for the others to be quiet. "Listen," he whispered. He could hear noises from around the bluff. There were no voices, just a few thuds and slamming noises.

His heart tripping in anticipation, Frank led the others around the bluff. When he reached the point where he could see the other side, he stopped again, holding the others back.

A large speedboat bobbed in the water, tied to a pier next to a small boatshack. As they watched, someone carried a wooden box from the shack onto the boat and disappeared belowdecks.

Using rocks and scrubgrass as shields, Frank, Joe,

Deb, and Cody crept toward the shack. But before they could reach it, the boat zoomed away.

Joe led the way to the shack. The door was padlocked. One window was locked, the other warped tightly shut. After a few minutes Frank and Joe pried it open, using sheer strength and Sergeant Chang's screwdriver.

A faint smell hit them immediately. It was the sweet sickening smell of meat that was old and going bad. It wasn't strong enough to make them gag, but it hung in the air, mingling with the fog that stole in through the window.

"There have been specimens stored in here," Cody said in a low voice.

"We get stuff sometimes from overseas that isn't cleaned well before it's sent," Deb told the Hardys. "This smell reminds me of that."

"Wood shavings—excelsior," Joe said, picking up a few shreds off the floor.

"Some countries still use this for packing. We get it sometimes with bones," Deb told him.

"Look, here's something," Deb cried out from the corner. She shone her flashlight on a piece of paper. It was shaped like a triangle, with two cut edges bordered in navy blue and one ragged edge.

Frank peeled the scrap of paper off the floor and

held it under his light beam. "It looks like a corner torn off some kind of label," he said.

"There's something on it," Deb pointed out. "A lowercase g and a number two."

"B-two-g," Joe said in a whisper. "The code at the mailing station," he said to Frank.

"Let's get back to town," Frank said. He was shot through with adrenaline. He felt as if he were straining to look at something from far away and if he could just get closer, he would see it clearly.

The four climbed out the window and retraced their steps down the beach and over the wire fence.

"We can catch Redwood Creek Trail over this way," Cody said. "It'll get us to the car quicker."

It took them half an hour, but they finally reached Cody's SUV, still parked safely in the eucalyptus grove.

Back in town, they picked up sandwiches for lunch, and then headed over to Skin & Bones.

There was a faint odor from the fumigation but not enough to bother anyone. They ate quickly, and it was two o'clock when they finished. Cody and Deb took the skull to the lab to clean it to see if they could find any identifying marks.

Joe got on the phone to check with Cody's network to see whether anyone knew anything about the boat-shack, *b2g,* or a missing human skull.

Frank booted up the computer in Cody's office to check online public records that would tell him who owned the beach property they had found.

No one made a connection that helped the case.

About three o'clock Dave knocked on the shop door, and Joe let him in. Cody and Deb came down, and they all gathered in the kitchen of Cody's flat.

"Man, it is great to get Mike Brando back behind bars, isn't it?" Dave said. "That weasel."

"Yeah, but someone else has to be helping him," Cody reminded Dave. He was interrupted by a loud tapping on the door of Skin & Bones. Deb let in a frantic Jennifer Payton.

"Cody!" Jennifer called up the stairs. "Where are you guys? I need you desperately. You've got to come over to help me finish getting set up. The dress rehearsal's in less than two hours."

"Remember, Cody," Frank whispered to his friend, "we're going to check her out while we're over there. Don't let her know how you feel—or even that you know about her buying your building or her plans for the future of this area."

"What's going on?" Dave asked. "Don't tell me you suspect Jennifer Payton of something."

"Cody, where *are* you?" Jennifer called again.

"Later," Cody said to Dave. "It's showtime."

Cody led the Hardys and Dave down to the shop. "Jennifer, I'm sorry," he said. "We're on our way."

"Okay," she said, hurrying back to the door. "Don't forget your costumes."

"Costumes?" Dave repeated. "Is this for the charity fund-raiser? Do you have room for me?"

"We always have room for more volunteers," Jennifer said without turning around.

Frank, Joe, Cody, Dave, and Deb grabbed the costumes Jennifer had given them and went next door to Reflections. The transformation of the club was wonderfully spooky. Under the black draped ceiling with red twinkle lights, cubicles were set up and connected in a mazelike pattern, almost like train cars opening from one to the next. Each had a scary scene inside. Visitors would be ushered through the scene and past the costumed figures, who would interact with them.

The Hardys and the others joined the gang of volunteers to finish setting up the scenes—ghostly parlors and attics, sunken ships, alien spaceships, witch kitchens, crazy scientist labs, caveman lairs, vampire crypts, werewolf forests, pirate cabins, and monster basements. All had been reproduced. When the setup was finished, everyone got in costume.

"So, what do you think?" Joe asked, flashing his werewolf fangs and stroking his hair-covered face. "Pretty scary, hmm?" He was dressed in his own T-shirt and jeans, but mats of hair hung out from under the long sleeves.

"Awesome," Frank agreed. He wore a neon blue jumpsuit. A pale green skullcap matched his alien makeup.

"So, when are you going to get in costume, Deb?" Cody asked as she emerged from the dressing room. She was an apparition in ghostly blue-white with pale fluorescent makeup.

"Very funny," she said with a crooked smile.

"Be careful or I'll make you walk the plank." Cody whipped off his large plumed pirate hat and made a courtly bow.

"What about you?" Cody said to Dave. "Did Jennifer decide you are so scary as Dave Cloud that you don't need a costume or makeup?"

"You *are* funny," Dave responded. "I was too late to be a character—I'll take tickets or something like that. But for the dress rehearsal, Jennifer is going to have some of us pretend to be visitors. We'll walk through the gauntlet to make sure you guys are scary enough to be fun, but not enough to cause permanent damage."

Jennifer also had choreographed surprising confrontations between some of the characters, which would take place on the stage in the corner.

The dress rehearsal filled the room with a jumble of howls, moans, screams, and cackles. Jennifer finally took the microphone. "Okay, everyone, time to stop. I want you to have plenty of spooky spirit left for tomorrow. Report here at four o'clock. But right now, let's party!"

Jennifer had planned a party with lots of food, music, and fun for the volunteers. The deejay fired up his sound system, and the music was deafening.

Frank, Cody, and Deb met up near Jennifer's office. "Have you seen Joe?" Frank asked.

"Not yet," Cody answered.

"He's still rehearsing with the vampire," Deb said. Werewolf Joe was locked in a wrestling match on the stage. He was acting out the skit Jennifer had cooked up, pitting the two most famous biters in horror history against each other.

"Okay," Frank said. "Jennifer's pretty distracted as it is. But you two keep an eye on her and keep her away from her office. I want to look around. When you see Joe, send him here."

Deb and Cody wove through the noisy crowd. Frank stood in the office door, but he couldn't take his eyes off the stage. "Come on, Joe," he muttered. "Get it over with. You can take him."

For a minute he was dazzled by what seemed like a thousand lights dancing around the room. He looked up to see a mirrored ball dangling and revolving from the ceiling. He thought of the piece of mirror that Joe had found on Cody's roof.

Then he remembered all the sports and fitness photos, awards, and certificates he had seen in Jennifer's office. He raced to the wall and scanned it eagerly. His eyes rested on one framed display, and he felt his pulse stop and then quicken. Hanging on the wall was a certificate attesting to Jennifer's championship karate skills.

"Excuse me," a young man said, coming into the office. Frank could hardly hear him over the noise. "Are you Jennifer's manager?"

"No, I just—"

"Tell her someone stole my costume," the young man said. "I was in the dressing room getting ready to change, and someone took it off the counter. It was the vampire costume she had made special for the fight with the werewolf, so she's not going to be happy about it. Had a full head mask and everything." He gave Frank a little wave and then rejoined the loud party.

Frank felt a wave of foreboding cascade through

him. "Joe!" he yelled as he left the office and focused on the stage in the corner. As he watched his brother struggling to take charge, the vampire got a stranglehold on Joe.

"Joe!" Frank yelled again, charging through the dense crowd. His voice was just one more in the crowd of party monsters.

14 Fear in the Fog

Frank barreled through the mass of costumed volunteers—some eating and drinking, some dancing. No one paid any attention to him as he yelled to Joe.

Still calling as he pushed through, Frank saw Joe dragged off the stage and into the wings. He spotted Cody and Deb and motioned them to follow him.

At last the three made it backstage. But neither Joe nor the vampire was there. Frank rushed to the back door of the club, a metal double door that led to a parking lot. One of the doors was being held open by a kickbar. There was no Joe, no car peeling away.

Frank went back in, saying, "Cody, call your dad. I

think Joe's been kidnapped. Deb, find Dave. We need all the help we can get."

Then Frank went to the deejay and told him to have Jennifer meet him backstage immediately. He also put out a call for Joe, just in case.

Frank paced the wings while the deejay's voice blasted through the sound system. "Jennifer, we have an emergency," he said. "Please report to the stage now. Joe Hardy, come to the stage."

Breathless, Jennifer was there in minutes. "What?" she said to Frank. "What's happening? Please—I can't take any more emergencies and disasters."

Quickly Frank told her about the stolen costume and the scene on the stage.

"Come on," she said. "So they fought and one of them won. It's over. They're probably out there scarfing up food now. Relax. Your brother will turn up."

"Listen to me," Frank said, his eyes narrowing as he glared at her. "This is not a joke. This is not a false alarm. Joe would have been here by now if he'd heard that announcement. He is either hurt and unable to respond or he's been taken away."

"What do you want me to do?" she asked. He could see the sparks of fear in her eyes.

"Were you on the roof of Skin and Bones Monday night?"

Jennifer's eyes widened and for a minute, he thought she was going to run. Then, still tense and looking as if she were going to sprint away any minute, she answered him.

"Yes, I was," she said. "But I wasn't trespassing. I own that building."

"We know that," Cody said, joining them. He turned to Frank. "Dad was out," he said, "but they'll find him. I also beeped him. He'll be in touch as soon as he can."

"I've been overwhelmed by this fund-raiser," Jennifer said to Cody. "Honestly, I wanted to tell you but decided to wait till this was over to sit down and talk with you."

"I know about your plans," Cody said. "And I bet they don't include my shop."

"Yes, they do," she said. She seemed to relax a little and not be so ready to jump away. "You're just the kind of quirky offbeat business I want to encourage here. In fact, I want you to move into the building on the other side of Reflections. It's bigger, and I'll let you have it at the same rent for a year if you'll stay."

"Why were you on the roof?" Frank asked.

"I didn't think anyone was in your building that evening. If Skin and Bones moves to the other side, I want to put a restaurant in your building, one with a rooftop café. I was just checking it out."

"But you attacked Joe," Frank said.

"Wait a minute," she said. "Is that what this is all about? You think because I kicked him then that I've done something to him now? You've got to believe me." Her tone changed as she pleaded. "I don't know what's happened to your brother."

Frank kept his eyes on her as she spoke.

"Monday night he surprised me and I panicked," Jennifer continued. "I didn't want to get into all this expansion stuff yet, so I just wanted to get away without being identified. I was defending myself. He was creeping toward me, and I didn't know who he was until I turned around. Then I pulled my kick so he wouldn't be hurt. Hey, I'm a champion. If I'd wanted to really hurt him, I could have. Is that how you figured out that it was me up there? The karate?" she asked.

"And a piece of mirror you left," Frank said.

"The mirrored ball." Jennifer nodded. "I've had trouble with pieces chipping off. I get them on my feet, and then I carry them around until I can reglue them. Look, if your brother's been hurt or kidnapped, I swear I don't know anything about it. But I'm ready to help any way I can."

Frank believed her. "I don't know of anything right now," he said. "Except report the stolen vampire costume and get the police here to interview everyone before they leave. Maybe someone knows the thief or saw him and can give a description. If you come up with anything, let us know or call Sergeant Thomas Chang, Cody's dad." He rushed out the back door with Cody and Deb close behind.

They raced through the parking lot, up the passageway between the buildings, around to the front, and into Skin & Bones.

Frank led them straight up to Cody's flat. He peeled off his jumpsuit and skullcap and washed off the alien makeup. Cody went into his bedroom to change. Deb stayed by the phone in the office, still dressed as a ghost.

"One of us has to stay here from now on," Frank said, joining her. "If Joe can call, he'll call here." He took out the triangular scrap of paper with *b2g* printed on it. He knew it held the answer, but he couldn't figure out how to break the code.

"Couldn't we call the bureau of public records and find out who owns that property with the boat shack on it?" Deb suggested.

"I thought of that," Frank said. "We've done it before in other cases. But in a metropolitan area of this size, it would take days to get the job done. They're always backed up with requests. We can have Cody's dad get the information for us much quicker. I wish he'd call—or better yet, Joe."

Like magic, the phone rang. But it wasn't Joe or Sergeant Chang. Dressed in a red sweater and jeans, Cody came out of the bedroom to take the call. When he hung up, he turned to Frank and Deb. "That was the dry cleaners," he said with a puzzled expression. "Joe's sweatshirt is ruined, and they can't fix it. But get this—it wasn't blood. It was a red paint glaze!"

"Why would Dave have red paint all over his jacket?" Deb wondered.

"The real question is why did he tell us it was blood?" Frank asked. He felt as if his mind was zooming around a track, circling and circling the clues. Then one of them jumped out at him. "Did Dave have a set of keys to your car?" he asked Cody.

"Sure. We both used the SUV for pickups, so I got him a set of his own."

"Did he ever return them to you?"

Cody thought for a moment. "Now that you mention it, I don't think so. Why?"

"Does Dave have a boat?" Frank asked as he turned to Cody's computer.

"Yes, he does," Cody answered. "I've never seen it though. Why all the questions?"

"You said Dave started an online auction site for computer equipment, right?" Frank asked. "What's his company's name?"

"ComputerCloud-dot-com," Cody said.

Frank typed in the name. Nothing came up. Then he typed *b2g*. Nothing. "Okay," he muttered. "Let's start with this." He typed *2g*. An alphabetical list of *2g* names started running down the screen: ads2get-results.com, ask2getanswers.com, attorneys2go.com, avocados2go.com.

When he got to the last two, Frank stopped the search immediately and refined his search. He typed 2go.

Again, a long list of names started cascading down the screen. The names starting with *a* tumbled off the bottom of the screen, and then the *b*'s started. He felt a quickness in his breath that matched the rapid pumping in his temples. There it was: bonz2go.com.

Frank read aloud. The website explained that this site was owned by Dave Cloud, also owner of ComputerCloud. Bonz2go auctioned hard-to-find animal, fish, bird, and human bones and other body parts.

"It's Dave," Frank told the others. "He's been sabotaging you, Cody. Taking your merchandise, intercepting deliveries, and selling them on the Internet."

"Deb, keep beeping Sergeant Chang until he calls," Frank said, grabbing his jacket. "Tell him we've gone to Dave's."

Frank and Cody raced to Cody's car. Cody was in shock but didn't doubt Frank's deduction. "It's a perfect setup for him," Cody said. "He's got all my contacts, all my network available to him."

"That's why we couldn't find him at the party tonight. He'd stolen the vampire costume to kidnap Joe."

"But why?" Cody said. "I'm the one he's trying to ruin." He drove the car up onto the Golden Gate Bridge toward Sausalito, where Dave lived. It was dark, and a thick fog was rolling in through the arches of the bridge.

"To get us off the case," Frank guessed. "Also, Brando was the perfect dupe. Dave could throw suspicion on him. Now that Mike's back in prison, Dave has to keep the idea alive that Brando has an accomplice on the outside."

Cody pulled into Dave's long driveway up a hill. "Turn off your lights," Frank said.

They drove up to the house, but it was dark and Dave's car wasn't there. "Where's his boat?" Frank asked.

They drove back down the hill to the marina. Cody parked a block away, and they ran quickly to Dave's pier and his boat. It looked like the one they'd seen that morning near the boat shack.

One light was on belowdecks, but there was no sign of anyone. His ears straining for a sound, Frank led Cody aboard. They circled the deck, then crept down into the cabin.

In the dim light Frank saw a dreaded sight. "Joe," he whispered, running to the corner of the cabin. Joe was tied and gagged, his horror makeup still intact. But they could hear his celebration "Yesssss" from behind the gag and werewolf hair hanging off his face.

A sudden dip to one side told Frank that someone had boarded. He pushed Cody into the head, and Frank jumped into the bedroom closet.

"Okay, we're ready now for our little jaunt," Frank heard Dave Cloud say. "I take care of you and that's one less person trying to figure out my profitable little scheme. Plus, the others will be scared off the scent once and for all. Sort of like killing two wolves with one stone—or should I say, rock."

Frank heard footsteps going back up to the deck. In minutes the cruiser moved out.

Cautiously Frank left the closet and motioned Cody to come out of the head. They freed Joe. "We can take him," Cody said in a hushed voice. "There are three of us."

"I agree," Frank whispered. "But we have to be cautious. He might be armed."

"I didn't see a gun," Joe said, his voice low. "But that's no guarantee."

"Okay, let's go on up," Frank said.

"Let's wait until we get out farther," Joe warned. "There's a lot of traffic here. We don't want an accident with other craft."

They waited until they could feel Dave increase speed. From the porthole they saw that they were farther out into the bay and cruising parallel to the Golden Gate. As they started up the companionway, the boat swerved.

Then it lurched and swerved again. For an instant, Frank thought they were going to ditch. They hurried up the companionway.

It was nearly impossible to see in the thick cloudy air. From their left they could hear the loud intonation of a foghorn.

Ahead, Frank finally made out Dave's form. "He's

in trouble," Frank murmured. Dave was grunting and seemed to be frantically trying to get control of the wheel.

"He's trying to turn," Joe said. "We've got to help."

A large dark shadow seemed to be racing straight toward them. Joe pushed Dave to the deck and grabbed the wheel, but it was too late.

With a gut-grinding boom, the boat smashed into the huge black mass rising out of the fog.

15 Rock On!

Frank woke up first. He was sore and tired but okay. His right wrist was twisted under him, but it didn't seem to be broken. His clothes were wet, and he was shaking with cold.

"Joe! Cody!" he called. As his eyes adjusted to the foggy night, he realized he was lying in a cave. Waves crashed against the rock wall below. Sea water washed into the cave, dribbling foam around the edges.

He scrambled to his feet and stumbled around in the dark. At last he found the others. Cody was lying on the ledge close to the cave entrance. Joe was outside the cave on a rocky outcropping above the entrance.

"Joe! Come on, wake up." Frank walked to where Joe was lying and gently shook his shoulder.

"Ummmph," Joe said, twisting his body as he woke. "The last thing I remember I was turning the wheel of Dave's boat. We were barreling toward this big—"

He stopped talking and looked up the rocky wall above him. Through the fog he saw lights in the distance, forming the pattern of a long bridge. "Whoa, we crashed into Alcatraz!" He sat up quickly and rubbed his hairy face. "I thought when werewolves wake up, they're back to normal."

"Ooooohhh," Cody called from inside the cave. "My leg's numb. How long have we been here? What happened?" He sat up and looked around. "Hey, are we on the Rock? In one of the caves? A prisoner tried to escape once and didn't get any farther than one of the caves. He finally gave up and climbed back up to the prison."

"Yes, that's where we are." Frank leaned back and looked up. "I can see the water tower and the top of the cell-block wall and the building itself. I can see the road winding up from the dock."

"You're right, Frank," Joe said, following his brother's gaze. The Hardys had been on a tour of Alcatraz on a previous trip. "It looks so small from the city," Joe said. "But it's big when you're on it."

"Is everybody okay?" Frank asked. "No broken bones, no bloody cuts?"

"Not that I can tell," Joe said. "Any cuts have been sealed by all this salt water," he added with a lopsided smile.

"I wonder how Dave is—*where* he is," Cody said.

Frank and Joe shook their heads. "I thought I saw a piece of the boat drift by, but it's so dark, I couldn't really tell," Frank said.

"It's so cold," Cody said, shivering. Another wave splashed at them as it hit the island's rocky wall.

"It's time to strip down for business," Joe said. He peeled the werewolf hair off his face and arms. "Okay, let's go," he said.

"We've got to get up on top," Frank agreed, looking for a place to start climbing. He began his ascent, gripping the rocky wall and hoisting himself up. "Come on, guys, find something to hold on to and someplace to put your toes. It's just like any other rock climbing you've done."

"Except for having no equipment and a wet wall covered with slimy seaweed," Joe muttered.

It took them about twenty minutes, but they finally made it onto solid ground. The dock was about forty yards away, and the cell block about a quarter of a mile up the winding road.

Frank checked his watch. "The night tour should be landing in about an hour," he said. "We can get a ride back with them. Let's go check in with the rangers."

"I want to find Dave Cloud first," Joe said. "I have a few words for him about dragging me away from a party."

"Okay," Frank said. "Let's look around a little. Now, if you were Dave Cloud, where would you go?"

"Well, he can't go to the rangers," Joe said, "because if I made it through the accident and can identify him as my kidnapper, he's busted."

"He probably can't escape," Cody said. "In the twenty-nine years this was a federal prison, practically no one made a successful escape."

"If he can't escape on his own and he can't ask for help, there's only one other choice," Frank said.

"What?" Cody asked.

"He's got to hang out near the dock and try to stow away on the evening tour boat to hitch a ride back to the city."

Frank, Joe, and Cody crept along the dark rock at the base of Alcatraz toward the dock. "Let's split up," Joe suggested. "The first one to find him, force him onto the dock. Then the other two will close off his escape routes, and he'll be trapped there."

Joe was the first to spot Dave. He was huddling in

the bushes between the road and the dock. "Hey, pal, how about finishing the fight we started at Reflections," Joe said. Startled, Dave jumped up. Joe pressed forward, and within minutes Dave had backed up onto the dock. Joe and Cody joined Frank, blocking Dave from leaving. He was trapped.

"It's either us or the water," Joe said. "And you sure don't want to join the rest of those prisoners who tried to escape from the Rock."

"I can't believe it's been you all along," Cody said.

"Hey, one way to handle competition is to get rid of it altogether, right?" Dave said, with a half-smile. "I wasn't just going to beat you," he told Cody, "I decided to bury you and put you out of business permanently. Then the market would be pretty much mine to rule."

"So you did it all?" Cody asked. "You trashed my office Monday night, knocked me out?"

"I did it," Dave said with a shrug. "Actually, I was just looking for some paper files. I have no trouble hacking into your computer files, but some of the first customers and dealers we worked with never got put into the computer. So I was after those."

Dave shrugged again. "You surprised me, so I had to drop you. The zoo packages were a nice bonus. I sold the ostrich skeleton and three anteater claws in an hour on bonz2go. I saved one anteater claw for your present," he added, nodding toward the Hardys.

"I got pretty sick of you two butting in, trying to track me down. Thought you'd get the message, but you didn't. That's why I kidnapped you." His eyes narrowed to snakelike slits when he looked at Joe. "I figured if you disappeared for good, your brother here would get the message and back off."

"You don't know the Hardys very well," Cody said with a snort.

"You intercepted Cody's overseas orders and left him the computer threats?" Joe asked.

"Sure," Dave said. "Actually, that was the easiest part. It was a great scam until you two came along. I thought I'd been busted for sure yesterday at the windmill."

"You called to lure Cody to the Polo Field," Frank said. "Why?"

"I was pretty well disguised, if you'll recall," Dave said to Joe. "I was going to threaten him, maybe beat him up a little and dump him. When I saw Deb show up, I grabbed her instead."

Dave looked out across the bay. "I knew you'd been following me earlier."

"You'd followed us first," Frank reminded him, "from Sergeant Chang's."

"Yeah, well, I've been keeping pretty tight surveillance on you all," Dave replied. "Like I said, with all the extra help from out of town—you two—I've had to increase my guard a little, make sure I know where everyone is."

"So you grabbed Deb," Joe prompted.

"Right. When I saw Cody's car, I knew either you or Cody had tracked me to the Polo Field," Dave said to Joe. "I knew you had seen me in the green car, and Cody's was just sitting there, empty. I still had my old keys on my ring, so I took it. I figured Deb had blabbed about the meeting, and for all I knew, there were a lot of people out there looking for me."

"So you hadn't planned to go to the windmill?" Frank said.

"No." Dave chuckled. "At that point, I was playing it by ear, you know? I was mad at Deb, so I took her out to the windmill. I was going to tie her up and gag her, then lock her up in there and just let her sweat it out till someone found her. The whole point of the afternoon was to warn the three of you off. I figured that would do the trick."

"She wasn't so easy to handle," Cody reminded him proudly.

"She sure wasn't," Dave said. "When she broke free and went out to the deck, I really got mad. Then when you showed up," he said to Joe, "I thought I'd had it.

But fortunately, you were more interested in saving her life than nailing me."

"And you never had a fight last night with Brando, did you?" Frank asked.

"So you found out about the red paint, hmm?" Dave said, shaking his head. "Actually, I did scrape my arm. I was coming over to meet you guys for dinner, so I thought I'd capitalize on it and throw some more suspicion Brando's way. I had you believing it for a while, I could tell. Why didn't you just throw that sweatshirt away like a normal person, instead of having it analyzed?" he added, shaking his head.

As Dave talked, the sound of a Coast Guard siren wailed through the fog.

"You know, I can forgive you for almost everything but devastating Bug Central," Cody said. "Letting all the beetles loose was the lowest."

"Not all of them," Dave said with a grin. "I kept the colony in the second refrigerator for myself. After all I need the little munchers, too."

"Not anymore you don't," Frank said. "You're going to be out of business for a long time."

"Was it your human skull that we found in Muir Woods?" Joe asked as the Coast Guard boat came nearer.

The look on Dave's face was one of real shock. "Muir Woods? You mean you know about the boat shack? You found the skull in Muir Woods?"

"We did," Frank said. "Did it belong to you?"

"Yeah, but I didn't know for sure where I'd lost it."

Frank could see the Coast Guard boat shooting through the fog toward the dock.

"I got stuck once at the boat shack when my cruiser wouldn't start," Dave continued. "My only choice was to hike out to the highway to try to hitch to Sausalito. I put two skulls and some other bones in a bag and started through the forest. It was late at night, pitch-black, no flashlight. I got all turned around, lost, fell a few times. With one fall, all the bones emptied out of the bag. The skulls rolled around, and I never found one of them."

"You just left it there?" Frank said, astonished.

"Hey, I just wanted out of that black woods," Dave admitted. "I get claustrophobic in that place. Besides," he said jauntily, "there were plenty more where that came from. I just had to hack into Cody's computer files."

The Coast Guard siren stopped, and within minutes they heard Sergeant Chang's voice calling Cody's name.

"Yo, Dad!" Cody yelled.

"Boy, am I glad to see you guys," Sergeant Chang

said. "Dave, I understand you've got a lot of explaining to do."

"He's already told us a lot," Frank said, "and is pretty proud of it all, it seems."

Sergeant Chang handcuffed Dave and read him his rights. Then they all boarded the Coast Guard boat for the trip back to the city.

"As soon as I got your messages, I called your flat," Sergeant Chang said on the cruise back. "Deb told me you'd gone to Dave's and why. When we got to Sausalito, we saw your SUV near the marina, Cody. I found out that Dave had a boat and that it was gone. I knew no one would take a boat out in this fog unless it was an emergency, he was crazy, or he was doing something illegal. When I called the Coast Guard to have them search for Dave's boat, I insisted they take me along."

"How did you know we were here?" Cody asked.

"The Coast Guard got a call from some fishermen that a boat might have ditched on Alcatraz. We headed here immediately. I was pretty worried until I saw you on the dock."

Frank, Joe, and Cody told Sergeant Chang about their conversation with Dave.

"Well, Frank and Joe, there's no doubt about it. You are definitely chips off your father's block. He's going to be very proud of you for putting Dave out of circulation. You were here on vacation, and you managed to save Cody's business in the process."

"Yeah," Cody said, giving the Hardys high-fives. "You might say your trip here has been a bone-anza for Skin and Bones!"

**Do your younger brothers and sisters
want to read books like yours?**

**Let them know there
are books just for *them!***

They can join Nancy Drew and her best
friends as they collect clues and solve
mysteries in

THE

NANCY DREW

NOTEBOOKS®

Starting with

#1 The Slumber Party Secret

#2 The Lost Locket

#3 The Secret Santa

#4 Bad Day for Ballet

AND

**Meet up with suspense and mystery
in The Hardy Boys® are: The Clues Brothers™**

Starting with

#1 The Gross Ghost Mystery

#2 The Karate Clue

#3 First Day, Worst Day

#4 Jump Shot Detectives

**THE CLUES
BROTHERS™**

A MINSTREL® BOOK

Published by Pocket Books

2324

Split-second suspense...
Brain-teasing puzzles...

No case is too tough for the world's greatest teen detective!

NANCY DREW®
MYSTERY STORIES
By Carolyn Keene

Join Nancy and her friends in
thrilling stories of adventure and intrigue

Look for brand-new mysteries
wherever books are sold

Available from Minstrel® Books
Published by Pocket Books

2313

Todd Strasser's
AGAINST THE ODDS ™

Shark Bite
The sailboat is sinking, and Ian just saw the biggest shark of his life.

Grizzly Attack
They're trapped in the Alaskan wilderness with no way out.

Buzzard's Feast
Danger in the desert!

Gator Prey
They know the gators are coming for them...it's only a matter of time.

A MINSTREL® BOOK
Published by Pocket Books

2023

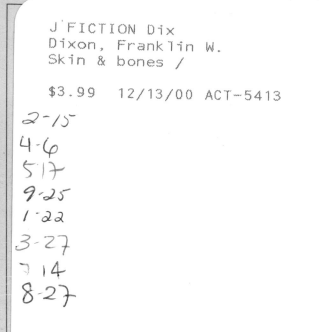

un-filled
ntures.

Published by Pocket Books

648-32